THE BOY AND THE SEA

Kirsty Gunn is the author of three novels, *Rain*, *The Keepsake* and *Featherstone*, and a collection of short stories, *This Place You Return to is Home*. In 2004, she was awarded the Scottish Arts Council Bursary for Literature. She is married and the mother of two young daughters. She lives in London and Edinburgh.

The Boy and the Sea

KIRSTY GUNN

faber and faber

First published in 2006
by Faber and Faber Limited
3 Queen Square London WCIN 3AU

Typeset by Faber and Faber Limited
Printed and bound in Great Britain by
Mackays of Chatham PLC, Chatham, Kent

The right of Kirsty Gunn to be identified as author
of this work has been asserted in accordance with Section 77
of the Copyright, Designs and Patents Act 1988

The author is grateful for the assistance of the Society of Authors
in the completion of this book

A CIP record for this book
is available from the British Library

ISBN 978–0–571–23019–8
0–571–23019–9

2 4 6 8 10 9 7 5 3

ONE

i

You know how sand pools cool in the shadows when you step into it from out of the sun? Yeah, well that's how he feels, I think, this boy, when he comes in out of the glare to the deep blueness of the shadows here. Like . . . It's relief, I think. To be out of the light in this place where the tall trees hang down their long branches, those twisty old pines that are broken up in parts, grown together back up behind the beach and everybody loves them, they say they do, but they don't go to stand amongst them the way he does.

'Cray-zeee . . .'

They don't love the same their deep darkness, their coolness and their shade.

There's the sound of voices coming to him from out across the water and it's what I have to start off with, how I'm going to begin with things here. These voices, and how he hears them, this boy Ward, how he hears the sound of his friends calling to each other, but from where he's standing it's like they're far, far away.

'Wretched, you are . . .'
    'My own man!'
    There's Alex.
    'Seriously, watch this . . .'
    And Jeff. And that other guy Richard brought up from the city.
    'No, you watch . . .'
    'Way!'

There goes Richard now, dabbing about like he always does. All of them together, some girls will be there. But with Ward apart from them, hidden by these trees, it's like, what are those kids doing really? Right now it seems hard to imagine. As though he's never known any of them before, to hang with, drip, to flat down the boards. Say, how's the tide, guys? Are we offshore? Be . . . You know . . . Like . . .

Out here . . .
    With me . . .

So he just stays where he is. He wants to, and not go anywhere else. He curls his toes and feels the sand crumb in all the little places, looks down at his feet, that feeling of your body seems remote from you, like it may belong to someone else. Still. Just to be here is alright. It's quiet and the tall trees are here, like they could be Ward's own grey and ancient pieces of wood. And there's that thing of how their grey barks are scraped back like to bone by the sea winds and long pine needles are scattered thick around the roots, piercing at his skin a couple of them but they don't hurt him. Ward hunches down and sifts through some strands of needle, sand, twig . . . Lets it sift through his fingers. *Frail*, it all is, is what the world is, his own body. If he was to think about it, what it is to be here and no one knowing, his body would feel scary in its lightness, like he might almost not be here, just some pieces of a boy, scattered, and fifteen not such a great age anyhow, he doesn't know anything much yet, could still let anyone take him into their arms, let him feel their fingers pulling down through his long hair.

That's what he wants now, actually. Like no words, no one else. Maybe it's because he's been coming to the beach here all his life is part of it, that it's the kind of place can allow you to be quiet. These few houses on the coast, on the eastern side of the island, and the physical part of it still gets to him, draws him to a kind of privacy he wants to keep. Maybe. Because things you know well you get to do that with, don't you, hang onto, like it's your own personal property and you've got some kind of special claim? Like those big old bleached ribs and spines of driftwood hunkered up along the sand further down the beach, and the cliffs on the northern side and rocks still drop from there when there's a storm out . . . All of it's known, he knows. Just the shape of the land even, that sweet crescent shape and the same old beaten-up looking houses where the same families have been coming, like his mother used to come with her family when she was a little girl . . . And the beauty of those houses too, of their kind of faded colours, and the colours of the sky and the flattened hills behind them . . . All of it, it takes Ward, it takes him. It gathers him in. And, of course, the sea.

Out here . . .

Always. That's what brings them, the families who come, to this curve of coastline where the sun rises up out of the waves at dawn and spreads itself all pink and red and yellow in the morning, sheets of colour on the water where the tides come in. Doesn't matter where you are, in shadows here or out at the edge, there's the presence of sea, like something right now waiting for you, watching. Like waiting for Ward now and watching, between the trees. And okay, he could say, he's here, okay? He's coming soon. Just wait for him, sea. It's not like it's going to be forever until he gets his board into the water again.

Through the trees now Ward checks again the glint of the way the waves are breaking, little chinks and low and even but a creel of white foam there, at the base of the cliff and there's a rise up past where the cliff juts out, like the water's backing into itself . . . And that's going to come to something later on. By five, say. It'll be banked and shifted southwards by then, a tidy wave for down on the lower beach, quarter of a mile or so out past Falcon's. He should let the others know. If he went out now, say, went back onto the beach where they all are, he could talk to them about it, how the day's looking, the tides, a feeling something's going to happen here, I don't know yet, change, but something, and yeah, he could talk to them about it.

The guys.
    Hey, guys.

Because that's what it's all about, isn't it, that the sea's got the whole surfing thing so down that she knows the kids can't help, some point, go in? It's the big reason here, supposed to be . . . For keeping up the boards. Talking down the weather. Some people who've been coming for years, surfing all through that time, say they know the sea so well they can read by the sun's reflection on the horizon what kind of swell will follow . . . In the end, it's not really about listening to the radio for the weather, or TV, but more to do with just being here, in the same place, summer after summer the same. The same blowy, still or rain-soaked air against your skin and how the sea will print against it. How you might place your board into the water and find that space for yourself, accommodation . . . Intuition, after all. I think so. For this boy. And for his father, for him, for sure.

So, yeah.

He should tell the guys.

Say, sure they've spent more time surfing off that farm bank coast than any other and could be another day for it today, easy.

Could be.

Yeah?

Oh, sure. Even if it's not great with the reef bank there and cut shingle when you come in, the waves are regular and old man Falcon will be cool, doesn't mind them hanging around on the edge of his land with the horses and whatever sheep he's letting run there . . .

And today. It could be the place, alright, come later, when that big tide gets down. They could all paddle out together from here but catch the inshore from round the corner and come in full quarter of a mile down past the turn . . .

But Alex doesn't like it. He says there's no vibe at Falcon's, and he's probably right. The beach is scratched-up looking from the farm stuff and the girls don't come. 'What are you thinking of?' is the kind of thing he'd say to Ward if he suggested it. Like why surf anywhere if there's no one around to watch you? Alex. Ward's best friend so you've got to take notice of him some point. In fact, Ward should probably just go back out onto the beach now and be with him, Alex, the two of them just hang out for a while, take their boards out maybe, but do nothing, think later about the wave and how they might plan it . . . They would have a nice time.

The water looks back at Ward from behind the trees and just thinking about it this minute, being out, the silk feel of the water in his fingers as he and Alex paddle lazy, talking a little maybe, the heat of the sun on his back, honey smell of wax coming up off the deck . . . Makes him feel . . . What? That he could be there right now? Like he really is there? It's something happens to him a lot, I think. That he gets so particularly in the midst of this place, in this world of sand and water and always talking about it, thinking about it, that it makes it just . . . Too vivid for him, somehow? Like he sees too much? Feels too much? And that's maybe why then he has these times like now of just having to leave all the other kids, the sound of them shouting out to each other through the waves and their transistor radios stuck in the beach and all of them playing different songs . . . Just leave, all the talk, all the hanging around and laughing and joking, and be on his own. Like those kids don't exist, like his mother doesn't exist, or his father, or his life in the city doesn't exist, or school, like none of it is counting for anything. Just be here instead, in these trees, so the thoughts of the water can come in on him and big, but there's space for them in this quiet, and you don't have to talk, act up in any kind of way. You just feel you could stay here forever.

But you can't, he can't. They'll be asking, where's Ward by now, going, you seen him? Dave, Charlie . . . Those guys from school. Jeff. Alex, by now, Alex might be asking. Anyhow, Ward should think about getting out there not for them but for himself, to show that he's not so different, so that no one even really notices if he's been gone. Really, I don't think he has a sense of whether his presence is taken in by the others or not. It's because of not talking much, being part of stuff while it's happening around you. And I don't know, why should it have to be so hard for this one boy when for other people it's just . . . Easy. Just living, or being together in some kind of nice group. Why should it need to fit together anyhow with having the right little words to say? It's just Ward finds it hard that way. Just him and it's not what people want. It's not what girls want. His mother calls him My Shy Boy and she runs her fingers that way through his hair and no words then . . . But it's not what most people want. His father keeps telling him, he should try to change.

Ward closes his eyes. Leans in against the trunk of the old pine, a smell like dust, but some green too, deep in.

And 'Where's Ward?' come the voices, he can hear them, Alex's voice.

'Way-oh-way!'

And he should be there, with them.

'Where is he?'

Because this is a summer place. Eastern side of the coast, black sand, and the tides . . . It's all supposed to be just easy, a holiday, okay? Like the heat is rising off the sand, hitting back on the side of the waves, one wave, another wave . . . And the sun is in the sky and the sky blue and the sun reflecting off it like it might reflect off a car you loved, stripped down and painted again, a car to take girls in, that kind of colour, for girls, and for the boys who drive them . . . And . . .

Easy.
　Yeah.
　Is how it's supposed to be.

Ward leans further in, puts his head back against the soft bark, turns the side of his face so he can feel the smooth of it against his cheek. But he can't stay here forever like a little boy. He's got to go. Tell Alex about the water he's seen, or tell all the guys, no big deal, what's going on there up at the cliff, it's something pretty good to say.
　'Okay,' go. 'So listen to me now.'
　Oh, man.

He closes his eyes.

Fifteen.

When you're a little kid you don't even consider this kind of stuff, how you are, how your parents are . . . But now. Ward doesn't want to open his eyes. Sometimes, I think, he can't come up with even a single word to say to his father that might be the right one. And his father talks, he talks. When the girls come round . . . Sitting outside on the front porch with the pile of books, and the way he looks at the girls over the top of his glasses, 'Who's this now?', pushing his glasses down the end of his nose, stretching his long legs out and those old faded board shorts he wears. 'What's up girls?' Those old shorts he always wears.

Ward keeps his eyes closed, tighter closing them, so it hurts, stings a bit, kind of. Only his mother calls him My Shy Boy. And she sounds way too private now when she does that. Better be careful when anyone's around the house if he's with her there. Be careful of anything his mother might do, say. The way when she might be thinking about something her hand will go out to him, the way she wants to pull him in. Sometimes she puts her arms around him and rests her chin on his shoulder, she's not even thinking about him but still he's taller than she is, and better watch out for it, that's all, because he's not a little kid. And he never used to think about these things, never, but now . . . 'Come here,' his mother says, turning her big wooden bracelet round and around on her wrist, resting one foot back against the side of the house. She looks at the two of them, Ward and his dad. 'Oh why don't you both just pick me up, you guys?' And then his father does that, goes over and picks her right up off the ground like she's just a little girl, and before they disappear inside the house, he turns, he winks at Ward, and he grins . . .

Well. No one needs to know this stuff, do they? What goes on, the way his parents are? The way Ward's father is? None of it is anyone's business, and you know what the sea would say.

Leave it, come here.

The waves glint and turn.

Come here to me.

ii

He should just get into the water. Stop thinking about all this, the sea's right: *leave it*. Ward opens his eyes. The light, the sky blue overhead when he looks up into it, blue between the green arms of the pines . . . It's beautiful and heat banking up now, it'll be good to go out there with Alex late morning or noon by now, near enough.

He straightens up, touches the tree near him one last time, that lovely grey wood. Then he makes himself break free. Just as quickly as he came out of the heat to the shadow so he runs back out now into the sun and the bright bleach of light and sky and water. There's the great long length of his stride as he goes. Over and over

15

the sand, like he's rising right up over the earth . . .
Runs, and as he runs the sand goes from cool to hot to
wet . . . Like black paint going through it . . . Back . . .
To the sea's edge –

'Look!'

Alex raises his arm.

'There he is!'

He's wearing a pair of sunglasses, tilted on his face in
a crazy way.

'Where've you been?' he says. 'It's a check-wave,' and
he points out a way, to a piece of the water that's just the
same, actually, as it ever was.

'I've been waiting for you,' he says.

There's a second, something passing between them, and
you can see, maybe, what I meant before. These two
kids who've known each other for . . . Ever. And how
Ward looks back at Alex now, at the crazy glasses . . .

'What have you been doing all this time?' Alex says to
him.

'Just –'

And they're only standing here.

'What?'

But Alex takes the glasses off, looks at Ward with his
own eyes. Like, what's going on, I mean, really? Tell me.
And it's that thing of the two of them looking in a

mirror, this moment. How boys are together, how brothers might be.

'I don't know,' Ward says.

Alex looks at him a second longer, and then he smiles, shakes his head. 'Oh, you . . . You're a weirdo, guy . . .'

So you see, it's true, it is there: he knows exactly what Ward means. They use the sea now as an excuse to look out to it, not to have to talk. Something about the way the colours of blue are collecting, the smoothness of the swell out beyond the line . . . Just look at the sea now. So what, for Ward, the others might be here, and the girls, that new girl who's here with Beth and Sarah and if Ward turned around now, if Alex turned, they'd be able to see them . . . Just be cool, there's the blue, there's the line. Even if it would be easy to turn around and look at those girls because none of them are looking over this way, stretched out on their towels . . . So what? They'll just be talking to each other, their heads resting on their arms and turning their faces to each other so they can hear what each other is saying, they're words Ward and Alex could never hear, none of the guys could hear, unless they were lying up there with them, they'd have to be that close . . .

'I know what you're thinking,' Alex says, he puts his hand on Ward's shoulder. 'But don't. There's no point to it, baby.' He laughs a brave fake laugh. Standing there with his feet apart, ankles dug in deep into the sand. 'Those girls . . .' he says.

'I wasn't thinking that.'

'Yeah, yeah.'

'No, really,' Ward says, and they have known each other for a long time, but he should get back into what's going on here, maybe start doing some of that talking he was planning on before.

So he says, 'I've got this idea.'

Points towards the cliffbase where he saw the thing going on inside the channel before. 'I think we should be getting into that, maybe,' he says.

Alex puts his glasses back on, straightens them this time. 'Where?'

'There . . .'

Ward can see, even from here, even after the little time that's passed, that his prediction is the right one. He's looking over a big, newly flattened piece of blue. The far sandbar has directed a thick channel of water into a kind of pool and pressure will be building, the tide coming from the north, a barely perceptible swell now, but the water dark and oily looking . . .

He traces out the shape of a wave that Alex can see.

'Get it? There to the right?'

The whole thing coming down to form what'll be a nice old-fashioned left if this stillness holds and the inshore comes, just a small break now, but building, heading southwards later on just like he thought, by five, on Falcon's, maybe even further up, make Alex happy, come straight in on soft, soft sand.

'See?'

The cliffs are quiet, no gulls stir there. It's like they're waiting, painted, the black drop falling into deep water. Alex probably can't see any of this, though, what Ward's trying to show. Like Alex would wait 'til he's in the channel before he even got up on a board . . . Well, that's not fair, but . . . Really, look at it now. The deepness of the smooth about an eighth out, it's like satin, like a slip of the water and some kind of lovely charge to it: Beauty. High time. How does Ward put it sometimes those days he has good days? Road to Ride?

'See?' he says again.

And you can, can't you, see? Or rather, sense it, a sea with something in it, like something's going to happen here, in the tides, the temperature? Don't all surfing stories do this to you, let you in on some kind of a big important wave? Like the next wave. Is going to be the best one. Long waited for. Something to pitch against – yet I'm not sure that's entirely what this day's about either. While Ward's dad's back at the house, and his mother's there with him, probably, the shutters in their bedroom closed, and when did anyone, anyhow, last see that man wet down a board?

But no time to think about that now. Alex has already turned away.

'See who's here!' he's calling out. 'And some news for us, okay?' He starts walking over to where the others are standing, and Ward must follow.

'Listen up,' Alex says.

The girls raise themselves onto their elbows, look over. This is the moment come to Ward, no turning back, of him being back here with the rest of them, having to find something to say, to join in. With every bone in his body articulated he feels himself there, presented, like just walking over with Alex then, to join Richard. Will. Rasfield, those guys in the year ahead at school . . . Like he feels every single inch of himself standing up here now near them, his arms hanging down at his side, his chest, these shorts he's wearing, every single inch he's aware of, Ward is, he can hear his heart. He's just standing here, a group of boys and girls, that's all he's doing, just here, standing on the hot sand . . .

'What news, man?'

And the girls are looking at him, then at each other. Like . . .

'So?'

And Alex is turned back to him, waiting, expecting . . .

'Well,' Ward says, takes a breath.

And they're just all here together, it's just that kind of group. He knows all of these people, he knows them, he knows about what he's going to say, the tide, what it's going to do . . . But . . . He thinks . . . It's like he can't think . . .

And then Alex says to him, 'No big deal, baby.'

Just quietly. Just to him, no one else hears it. *No big deal.* And Ward looks at him, yeah? Like, really? Is this okay? And the girls get up off their towels. They stand, push their hair back, put their sunglasses on.

    'What's happening?'
    'You guys thinking about going out?'

Beth. Sarah. The new girl, all standing quite close to him, looking at him, waiting, and . . . Really. Could Alex be right, could this just be okay? Ward takes another breath.

Then he says, 'The water's showing a deep pull about a quarter out, by the cliff I saw it. Means a change of temperature, probably, further out at sea . . .' and he points, and there, you see? It is okay. He's started and he can keep going now, tell them about the weather report he heard, that look of the smooth that means a seam of deeper water come in . . .

And Alex smiles, nods his head, fine, this is what Ward does just fine, and he's right, isn't he, Alex, it can just be easy. The guys come in, listening and Ward keeps talking, and all of them are gathered around him, friends, that's what they are, remember, all of them together here.

'What time, Wardy?'

'Later,' Ward says. 'Maybe five.'

'Okay.'

'Okay.'

'Thanks for that, man . . .'

'Sure,' Ward says.

'So what'll we do 'til then, people?' says Jeff.

And Sarah says, 'Beth's already got an idea.'

And so, it is okay. Can be. This feeling of these people here, and Ward knows this feeling, it's familiar. The whole thing, how everyone's parents know each other's parents, their schools and where they live . . . The whole thing. It's like . . . Connection, you know, and Ward standing here, with the rest of them, like he belongs, really, because he should belong, shouldn't he, to this kind of group, and they're all close together here and there's an arm, close to his own arm, and a voice, just to the right of his shoulder, 'Hi.'

The new girl, and she smiles.

'You're Ward, aren't you?'

'Yeah.'

Her face is turned towards his, the sun reflecting off the pale tint of her glasses.

'Okay,' she says, the girl says. Then they both look out across the ocean.

It's so beautiful there, but Ward . . . He doesn't know what to do. He has the girl's arm next to his, touching actually, and the side of her body is there, near him, but his own arm hangs like a giant lump of wood, like suddenly he can't move at all, or maybe he thinks if he moves even one inch he'll knock into this girl or she'll think he's doing something weird, so he keeps that whole side of his body really still. If he could just think of something to say. Find some words, say something just to her, that she might understand. Like the water out there, the miles out there of blue and green . . . To say all kinds of things about the water, and being in the water, and what it is to surf the water . . . To show her somehow. Maybe put his arm around her, who knows, tell her . . . About the pull he feels for the waves, the rips and the tides, and maybe she would say to him, that's amazing, Ward . . . And he would go on and on, with these phrases and words, describing with such fullness the feel of the ocean when you're out that deep, the salt, how it's like a body holding you . . . If he could just find the words, the right words . . .

But instead he says, 'I reckon we could do something with that. It's coming from the north, my dad said . . .'

And the second those words are out, the awareness with the girl is gone.

No.

The sea sighs, falls away.

No.
No.
No.

But it has, the feeling's gone. Something about saying that, his father . . .

No.

Too late, it has. Happened like it always does, the mention of his father's name. So Ward's not the one here but his dad, may as well be, may as well be him standing here. Like it's only him that counts, his words about the water the words Ward himself's ended up using, turning the whole thing into some kind of story his dad would tell, with facts in it, that kind of power. Is it exactly. The way his father talks about the sea, like to control it, and Ward listens and now look at him, he's doing that same thing. Like the guys are always asking 'What does your dad think?' when they're not sure if they're going out or not. 'Did your dad see the water you're talking about, Ward? What does he say?' So Ward's swept back to thinking about the ocean now but in his father's way. So that when he does look out to sea again the view before him's not his own any more, that's gone, it's only his father's plan for the day spread out before him now.

And something more serious there. Okay. The way the tides have collected more full, than Ward first thought. It's true. From that water at the bar to the right of the cliff, and beyond that, further out, where the reef drops away . . . You can see. That any little thing that happens now, change of temperature, even the slightest part of that storm last night . . . How it's going to make the water thicken, go dark and a wave come. *'A norther.'* He may as well have just said the word to the girl here but she's turned away, 'a norther', because that's what his father calls it, when that happens, that mix of temperature drop and a decent inshore. Like it's something to be scared of but his father's never been scared, he just smiles. Like he smiled this morning after he spoke about the weather, before he went into his room to the computer. 'Watch yourself little boy,' he said.

Well . . . So what? Big water's always good to talk about and who's scared, Ward's not scared either. He turns, sees his board where he left it, the long shape, green and white stripe but faded now by outings, the salt, the sun. He can still make it okay here. He wanted something really good to go out on and so it's a norther, so what, he can manage that, he can make himself manage, and without his father too.

Forget about his father. He's reading now, or making money on the screen. He's not even anywhere near this ocean. It's Ward, his friends who are here, who we're thinking about now . . . This girl who said Hi to Ward, whose arm touched his arm . . . So don't let it come back now, every crazy little thing his father does. He just said something this morning, that's all, when he was sitting at the table in the sun. 'What are your plans this morning?' Taking a sip from his coffee he just looked at Ward over the rim of the cup. 'You going into the water?' Then he put the cup down. He just talked about the weather. And that could be all there was to it, okay? The window open. The table. The newspaper. The whole thing in sun. And just talking. About pressure, a big storm fifty miles out at sea the night before, expect part of it to come back in. 'Okay,' Ward kept saying. 'Okay.' There was wind speed. Temperature. Count-waves to justify. 'Okay. Okay . . .' Then his mother came in. She sat down and poured coffee, and right there his father stopped. That was it, all over, when his mother came in because then it was just the two of them together again drinking coffee, like every other morning, looking at pages from the paper, and Ward was left standing there. Standing, like waiting, kind of. For . . . what? There was the table. The newspaper. Just the same as every other morning, his father sitting there with his mother and their feet in a tangle together under the table yet still Ward was waiting, somehow . . . Standing there . . . Then finally Ward's father said, 'So?' And suddenly it seemed like hours since he'd told him all the other stuff, the radio report, the storm. Hours since the two of them had been together in that way, his father talking to him, just him . . . Because he just said then, 'You ready? Prepared?'

Then go, he means. Because I don't want you here.

But you know what? So what? That's just more information, more words okay, but nothing new, and his father good at that . . . Making the words seem more important than they need to be so just forget about anything that man says. He doesn't even go out any more. When did anyone last see him? Less and less going to the shed where his big guys are, those old nine footers he used to use all the time but he doesn't use them now. He's just words now, and just because Ward had stood there, like some kind of fool still waiting for something like a king might give him something . . . You don't have to keep going over and over it, okay? Because the minute his mother came in of course his dad turned away. It's what they're like, the two of them. That look they give each other. His mother reaching up her hand to say to Ward 'Good morning, darling,' but looking at his father while she did it . . .

That was this morning. And forget about this morning now. He's with Alex now, and there's this girl, too, Alison, Beth's friend. And Beth's here and Sarah and Richard and Will . . . It's all here, he's here. Here's the beach, towels spread out, bags. Here are the little radios buzzing away in the sand. Some umbrellas are up further down, some little kids playing. And the water, just . . . Hanging. Like a veil, that's what Ward thinks and nothing to do with his father, that's what he would have liked to say to Alison before. Just how the water's like a curtain on a stage and about to be pulled back to show them the whole thing, like he could see that all his hopes are out there behind the curtain, so it could be pulled back to show that there's nothing he need be frightened of or ashamed of, uncertain about. Nothing there that he need think is so different from the rest, or strange that he couldn't show to himself, to this girl who's arm touched his arm: Like, see? It's okay. It can't devour me. A veil. It pulls and covers. Each wave a piece of the blue to cover, rumpling itself, smoothing, wrinkling into waves and spreading out again, a curtain but nothing behind it to fear only all your hopes, only everything you ever thought you wanted.

iii

'We doing something here?'

Ward turns round and Alex is looking at him, waiting.

'We going out, or what?'

'I guess . . .'

But listen . . .

'I guess . . .'

It's his father again. And: Guess nothing, is what he would say. You're no god to guess, only know. Even with Alex here, the rest of them, he can't kick the stuff with his father.

'Come on, Ward!' Remember? 'You can do it!'

All that. Right from the beginning.

'I know you can.'

Yeah, yeah, Ward knows. Putting Ward up on his old long-board when Ward was still this little kid, only learning to walk and his father had those big hands of his around his waist to steady him.

'That's it! You're doing well, Wardy!'

And then he's older and his father's bringing him in alongside, laughing at Ward every time he got scared and the wave brought him down, 'Don't worry! There's nothing to be scared of' . . . So never once say 'I guess', because you don't guess, with that kind of father, you only know. He's fixed it. That the water has you in check and you're part of that, no discussion, and you don't guess, ever, just do it, you have no choice, only go out with your father and you want to, you can't do anything else.

So yeah, yeah, of course.

'I want to be proud of you!'

That's his father right there, the way Ward used to always see him, his body laid flat, paddling out, using those arms, those same hands that were placed around Ward's waist once. Same eyes, looking at Ward this morning, blue eyes as blue as the water here. Watching him, testing him. 'You going out?'

'Your dad,' Alex says. 'He's the man.'

Suddenly Ward looks really tired.

'We could go,' he says to Alex now, but really, I think all he wants to do, this second, more than anything, is just go home to bed. Pull the curtains closed. Lie down on cool sheets and let the day pass, let it pass. Nothing to do about thinking or swimming or feeling the sun's burn on your skin . . . Just sleep . . . So everyone thinks his dad's so cool, they don't know him. Doing all that stuff on the computer, it's just money, or reading on the front porch, that's all he does now. Click, click. The market, and 'Hey, girls' on the front porch. He doesn't even get up any more on a board, just click, click, even on holiday, all his money while the sea's there, the weather, but his father stays right where he is. So he tells stories about the water, it's only when he feels like it, gives out these special facts . . . Mostly he contains things. Ward's seen how it works. The way people act around his father, even if they've known each other for a long time still they listen up, pay attention, and the kids do that, 'Mr McFarlane, sir . . .' And all because his father makes them behave that way. Like this morning, the way he uses silences, then words, it's control. Acting like he's not anyone's father. Like Ward's mother might come up to him, and she'll put the palms of her hands down flat upon his bare flat belly, and he says to her, 'What's your name again? You're pretty. Can I go out with you?'

Well . . .

So Alex says, 'The man.'

Alex doesn't get Ward's dad now, he gets him.

'And I say we go check things out.'

Because, listen. He can't think about this stuff forever. It's day here, it's this day, and more to do in the sunshine than sit around thinking about his father all the time.

'Yes! Yes!' Alex grins back at him, raises five.

'Come on then,' Ward says, and he walks over to his board.

Anyhow they'll go through the motions. Is what I see happening here. Nothing much going on out on the water now but that was always going to be later and for now it's decent enough for Ward just to be here with his friend, his nine-line stuck back against the low dunes, waiting. Ward gets up close to it, it needs some work. He runs his hand across the front, later this afternoon he'll do it. Take it in, melt the wax down a little in the sun. Use that softest cloth. There are these little abrasions here, and here . . . He can smooth them in with wax before he goes out. He twists the lead which needs new but it'll hold for today. Twists it again, yeah. It'll hold fine, should do.

'Okay?'

There's Alex's voice just behind him, Ward turns, he's already carrying. And the girls are looking over now.

There's that girl again, Alison . . . But it has really gone. The feeling. Something about it wrecked on the words of his father before and that stuff, 'You ready? You prepared?' Maybe he should have just picked up the whole table, brought it down. Yeah, right. Like he would have. Broken through the wood and his parents there, disclosed that naked tangle of their feet . . .

Come on now, leave it, says the sea.

And he should leave it, forget about it . . .

Come on . . .

But his mother knows, doesn't she, exactly what is going on. The way she said to Ward's father this morning, 'Robbie, what are you doing to him here?' and then his father left the room . . .

The sea softens, pushes forwards, gently on the shore.

She knows.

And now Alex is saying, 'What are you waiting for?' and Ward realises he's just been standing. He looks at Alex and Alex is smiling, easy. Like he always is. Best friend, you know. The easy one. A reminder, somehow, that in the end what we've got here, no matter what else is going on, these two boys on the beach right now, surf- boards under their arms, going out together even though there are no waves, just going out in the sun, on the water, and have a nice time, guys, have a nice time.

'So?' Alex says.
   'So?' Ward says back.
   'Let's do it.'
   'Let's do it.'

They start walking together towards the water. Behind them, the girls are there, they're calling out:
   'Take it easy, you two!'
   'Yeah, be really careful out there!'
   Laughing, 'Yeah, impress us, please! Out on the flat calm!'
   'You going to hold each other's hands?'

And, you know? So what if he did take Alex's hand? Just take his hand. They've done it before, used to. When they were little kids: like saying to each other, Can we stay together? Will you look after me? Like Ward watches the little kids look after each other on the beach now, picking each other up out of the water, the bigger kids saying to the little ones, C'mon. I'll show you how.

Ward hears the girls still calling out, 'Bye guys!'

But Alex doesn't stop walking.

'Bye girls!' he just yells back at them, then says to Ward, 'They're only jealous.'

'Yeah?' Ward looks back and all he sees is they're lying down on their towels again, not even looking at him and Alex, just at each other. One of them, Beth, is putting lotion on Sarah's back.

'I don't think –'

'Oh sure,' Alex cuts in, by now he's walking on into the water. 'They wish we'd asked them to come along for the ride, that we might tow them out, you know? So they can get a suntan lying up on our boards . . .'

Ward smiles. There's Alex up ahead, and of course he can't look after Ward, in the end, though he might act that way. They're two boys, that's all, and not for years will Ward think about any of this that's going on right now, him and his friend, how they were once. Maybe even years later he won't think about it, or won't put it into these kinds of words. How it was that Alex used to make things easier for him when he was a boy, like 'Bye girls!' Turning it into some kind of joke. Making it for Ward that all the other stuff going round and around in his head shouldn't matter either, no big deal, remember? That's what Alex said.

He's walked further out by now, Ward has, into the water. The beach feels far behind. There's that way the sun blanks everything out like a photo too exposed and it does that now, blanks out details, edges, like it might blank out any thoughts. Ward squints up his eyes. The sun goes into a melty blur and mingles in the water. Alex is already pushed in and up onto his board and in this light he's like a piece of pale colour against the white of the sea. Ward walks deeper, the sand smooth liked it's carved beneath his feet. There's the weight of the board under his arm but wave-height now and he releases it. He puts his arms out together, head down and slips into the water, comes up against the board, pushes it under him. The sun is instantly hot on his skin. On his back. His shoulders. It's all just sun, they're caught in it, all of them. Himself, his friend, the people on the beach. Sun. Like that kind of photo. Alex up ahead, flat down on the board and strong looking, even though he's blanked out too into sun and colour, this light, he's strong, he's young and safe.

Ward starts to paddle out to catch him up, Alex turns. Now he's closer Ward can make him out clear. It's like the image has magnetised in the exposure, giving out-lines, details . . . Alex's dark hair slicked down on the back of his neck. The colours of his wrist strings, pink and yellow and bright green flicking in and out of the water. Ward comes up alongside.

'Hey.'

'This is nice.'

'Yeah, it's pulling. It's easy.'

They let the water play against them, one-two, one-two, the motion of the swell.

'You okay?' Alex says.

Ward dips his hands against the slap.

'I reckon.'

They don't even have to do much work here, the tide's taking them over towards the bar, the breakwater just . . . Whoa, there . . . And they're over.

'Yeah.'

'Wow.'

Always that nice feeling of rising up and coming down, back off the other side and now you feel like you've entered the ocean.

'Wow,' Ward says again, feels a deep breath come out of him. There's the slip, slip sound of the water up beside him, clear sides of blue and the deep rhythm beneath that's navy and dark and true.

'I'm pleased we came,' he says.

'Me too.' Alex turns over on his back. Puts his arms up, brings them down. Then he says, 'Why were you going to leave before?'

Ward looks at him.
'Leave?'

There's a beat, a second. Then . . .

'C'mon. Don't bull me, man.' Alex closes his eyes. 'I knew you were thinking about it,' he says. 'When the guys came over, you were thinking about running again. Just then, and when the girls were there.'
'That was before.'
'No later, when that girl –'
'Alison,' Ward says.
'Yeah.' Alex leans over and flicks Ward's back. 'She likes you.'
'Yeah?'
'Yeah.' Alex lies back, closes his eyes again. 'You know,' he says, 'Beth's got something later we could go to.'

But just then a rise of slow water comes up, right under, lifts them both and swings them out, far up left. The boards separate. Alex is there, pulled back pretty much to the same place, but Ward's swell's still taking him, he drifts, goes out a way, then holds. A gull wheels over-head. Ward sees the red on its yellow beak, that mark like a bit of blood, and the cry coming out, Arghh! Arghh! It's that close. He puts his head back so there right above him is the bird's white underbelly, the soft nap of those feathers, and then the whole shape arrows straight down into the sea. The swell lifts again, dips, and the bird's up again, a slice of something in its beak, the bird can't manage it. It drops back into the water, a big enough fish, so, yeah, he was right. Of course. His dad was right. Big fish in the channel come from way out in the ocean and too big for the gulls here to feed on, means . . . New water. Ward smiles, maybe with feel-ing the energy of it, where it's come from, it's in the gull's cry. There was the moment of the swoop, and the blood real on the yellow bill as the fish was taken . . . New water alright.

'You see that?'

Ward comes up alongside Alex again, but Alex hasn't noticed. He has his eyes closed like he's sleeping, and the sky's quiet now, the gull gone. Ward watches him for a minute or so, the way he just lies there, this little smile on his face like he's sleeping. Ward could do with some of that kind of chill-out, hang. Why not close his eyes too and relax. Then, just when he does that, lays his head down on his arms . . . Alex says, 'We should go. Her parents are away for the day. She's inviting people around. Like drinks, like a lunch . . . Everyone's going to be there.'

Ward unfolds his arms.

'We should go,' Alex says again.

He paddles a little, then brings his arms up, out of the water and places them, one on top of the other on the board in front of him again. Rests his chin on them, looks straight out ahead.

'Well?' Alex says.

And the blue is there, above the brown of his arms, a close horizon a couple of feet out, no more. And he can smell the salt water on his arms, licks the back of his hand for the taste, and . . .

 'Well?' he says back.

I think it's all he can do.

Not really answer, I mean. Like just act as though this isn't a big thing, that he doesn't care whether he goes to some party or not, when really . . . Why should he have to think about anything else? When he's out here and all his world is here? Go inside to some party, to sit around in the dark?

But.

Alex has said it now, and maybe he's right, that they should go. Like if everyone else is going to be there and it would be too weird if he didn't join in. If he stayed out here, say, never went to Beth's place, just stayed . . . Sounds nice to me. He closes his eyes.

  'Ward?'

  Then he says, 'I guess.'

Alex lets out a laugh.

  'You "guess", huh?' he says, he laughs again. And then, a few seconds pass and he starts humming that old Elvis Costello song.

  A–li-son . . .

It's where all the jokes come in, now, of course. This thing of all the kids getting together and the girls, what's going on . . .

Ward smacks at Alex across the water and Alex gets him right back.

A–li-son . . .

Smacks him again.

And it's exhausting, actually, that this is the way they're supposed to be doing things now. Like everything's some kind of little act and you talk, or make some joke or other to cover what you really want to try and say. He riffles some more water over at Alex because Alex is giving him this kind of look, and still humming, like yeah, yeah . . . This is what it's all about. Like when he put his arm around Ward's shoulder before, 'I know what you're thinking.' But what? Ward himself doesn't know what he's thinking. Half the time, so what does that mean, Alex acting like he can guess? It's feeling, that's what it is, not thoughts. Like feeling behind his heart now, the memory of that girl's touch, Alison's, the feeling of her arm against his arm, standing beside him back there, it's that stuff all jammed up inside him when Alex was asking about this party and humming that dumb song . . . Not thinking about girls and sex. They all talk about that, at school, all the guys, so it can't be that, no. This is more like . . . Being winded. Like breaking in the tunnel and losing it and managing to get back on the board but only just, like nearly losing everything when the wave started by being so clean.

A–li–son.

'Cut it out,' Ward says to Alex, but Alex keeps on humming.

A–li–son.
  You-know-
  this-pain-
  is-ki–lling-meeee . . .

'It's boring, you know?' Ward moves the board away.

Because how does anyone, anyhow, know what to do? Girls? The whole thing? He dips his finger in the water. In their swimsuits. Girls. At the front of his family's house, a whole bunch of them. The way they come wrapping around the house when his dad's sitting out front on the porch, stretched back that way of his in his broken down old wicker chair and just alone there mostly, his books, his legs stretched out . . . And –
  'What are you reading Mr McFarlane?'
  'Well, what are *you* reading, sweetheart?'

No one has any idea. What it's like. To have a father out alone there on the porch, your mother off somewhere, being on her own somewhere so the girls come around . . . In their little swimsuits, standing around in front of his dad, drawing with their toes on the soft old wood of the porch, trying to be shy. Oh, Alex . . .

A–li-son.

You've no idea. The way they're talking to his father, what they're doing at school, what they're reading and his father going 'That so, honey? You think that?', listening to them like he's interested in every little thing they have to say.

No one has any idea, not really. What it's like being around it, this kind of thing his parents give off. His father sitting there, and those old shorts on but that's all he wears . . .

And Ward can imagine, oh yeah, what his father would say.

'Now who's this?' Pushing his glasses down his nose, looking over them.

'Alison, hmmm?'

Putting down his book. 'That's a very nice name.'

It's not fair. To have so much, like his father has so much but still he wants to take more. Like it's not enough to have the shutters closed and Ward's mother with him . . . Still he wants more. The sun beats and burns. Already it seems like a million years ago Ward was standing in those cool trees. He feels the board beneath his belly, his chest, looks out over his arms across the blue. Really, it's not fair. Because Alex may think his father's so cool but he doesn't have him for a father.

Ward lets his head rest easy on his arms. The sun, hot. The water, slap-slap, edging the board.

They've no idea, any of them.

Slap-slap, goes the water, gentle.

And the way I hear it, right now, it's like it's holding him. Keeping him. That sound, the sea. Curl of white at the edge of a wave turn, that kind of crack in the water that's going to come later this afternoon, but for now . . . The sea . . . Where the sea comes from, goes . . . Ward closes his eyes . . . And this is how the sea goes . . . Early morning . . . What she does . . .

Early morning

Starts by saying this same thing, over and over:
  I am. I don't change.
  Makes her way upon the sand.

It is early morning, same day we're talking about but so early, before the boy is at the table with his father, the words exchanged, and the light is barely come in across the water but it's starting now, that slow, crazy-slow slip of the dawn coming up over the edge of the horizon and making the sea turn, swell, move herself towards the sun.

I am.

Shells lay clean along the water mark, like ornaments, their shapes and colours, their delicate thin and broken pieces lain embedded in the soft wet of the sand.

49

And here's the boy's mother come up behind him on the shore.

'It's early,' she says. 'Why are you here now, when you're young, you should be sleeping . . .'

She might come up to him, put her hand upon him. To that part of his shoulder there, that part of a boy where, though you're fifteen, still the bones stick out like the nubs of wings.

'You should be sleeping . . .'

And can you feel it, know what it's like, to be a boy and have your mother come upon you this way, put her hand upon you, on the back of your neck now and you close your eyes and . . .

Only me.

Early morning, and the water gentle. The boards can wait. The sea crumbling, crumbling at her edges. The sea pulled under with her own tides, pale blue and rose upon her skin, the colours of the dawn.

'Come inside,' says the woman, the mother, the wife. 'It's too early . . .' and the boy turns, to follow, as the sea waves pull, another piece of the day, seconds, minutes, another wave, another wave . . .

'Come on,' the woman says, the mother says, while the sea says Come with me, 'Come with me,' and he goes, the boy goes.

TWO

i

When they get back, Ward and Alex, the beach is empty.
The kids have gone, like noon, High Noon in a movie,
the sun right up overhead and no shadow, there are no
shadows here.

They come right in, stash their boards in the sand, don't
even sit down, because they're late already for this thing,
probably, Beth's, and Alex wants to go on straight away
but Ward's going to need a few minutes. More than a
few minutes actually it's going to take, he's going to need
a bit of time here. There's a sense of something begun,
this thinking about his father, how his father is, like a
kind of a story but his father's real, you know, the stuff
is real.

So he says 'See you' to Alex.

Alex looks back at him, a kind of look that says, what's this all about, but that doesn't change anything. Ward's staying, he's not leaving right away.

Then Alex says, 'You.'

He gives Ward a little poke into the shoulder, then turns, starts off down the beach. Ward watches him go. He's on his own again.

What he wanted, sure, but suddenly the beach looks lonelier than it did before. All the stuff with his father's left him washed out somehow, though he should be used to it by now, thinking about his father, watching him. I guess all that started long enough ago.

'You do it like this, see? Watch me.'

Like a first memory, kind of, like he was thinking about before. Ward maybe two years old, and his dad taking him out onto the water, to sit him up with him on the board.

'Like this.'

Is how it began.

'Better, hold onto me now.'

The lessons, instructions.

'Are you watching?'

Over and over.

54

'Are you watching me now?'

His father fixed that way, wilful, in his set against the water.

'I just want to see you do it,' he used to say.

'But I don't want to.'

''Course you want to,' he used to say. 'Copy me, Wardy. 'Learn it so you're just the same as me.'

So sure, that's where it begins alright, and Ward's dad that way because he'd been that kind of kid himself once, taught by his own father, and hard. This was back on those long, fierce, east-facing beaches you get up north and it's so different there where you're full-suit most of the year for a start, his dad's told him, and the waves with this kind of . . . Glacial stillness. Like they seem to wait and wait for you out there in the cold and then, only when they're ready, not when you're expecting them because there's no pattern to their movement, they just wait and then let themselves crack, wide open with a fury, headed straight in for the beach. And in height. Those waves. Temperature. In winter great chunks of ice might be in them, you went out far enough, and at night, in that little cabin on the beach where Ward's dad used to stay with his father . . . He'd hear the blocks crash sometimes as the waves broke. As they broke and thrashed in a million little pieces on the shore.

Okay.

So there's that. To begin with.

The million little pieces.

Part of Ward's history right there, first part, but his father didn't stay up north with his dad for long. He came south, left that old man, you know, when he himself was still just a kid, hitched a ride, I suppose, something like that, and that's when he met Caroline then.

C-

Ward starts to write her name on the sand . . .

Because she's another beginning, really, his mother.
    He does the a the r a funny kind of o . . . -l-i-n-e . . .
    It's all because of her, his dad meeting her one summer here, both kids but it starting up between them, another kind of story just the same and water in it, too, of course, because no one knew what they had, Ward's dad always said, well they knew, but they didn't use the waves here like he did until he came to show them how.

And he was fifteen.
    C-a-r-o-l-i-n-e.

This good-looking kid coming in on the scene here, right up on the edge of his board and coming straight towards her. Of course you can see how it must have figured. How he must have looked, as Ward's mother stood on the beach watching him, that he was coming in for her, somehow, his arms held away from him like some kind of an angel.

C-a-r-o-l-i-n-e.

I can see it, alright.

From the outset, Ward's father says, he knew. Like the water, she was the one belonged here. There was her family who'd been coming to this same place on the coast but the minute he saw her, that same day when she saw him coming in, and the light on the waves around him so bright in reflection he couldn't even make out her face but something . . . He knew. Like Ward would have known, his father used to tell him, if he'd come upon his mother in the same way, that she was part of everything here, the sand hills and flat grasses, all the sea inlets and waves and coves . . .

So, yeah.

Ward looks at the letters he's made.

His mother the beginning of the way it all worked out

here. Because Caroline's father used to get up okay, there were a bunch of them in those days had been regulars on those wooden boards they used to have back then, these older guys, but still it wasn't until Ward's mother fell in love with his dad that surfing became something people talked about, wanted to do. Because he showed them, he got them started. To be serious about the water and it being about more than just going out, you know, it was your spirit.

No wonder Ward's dad goes on and on about the water still. It's what he used from the start to win himself a place here among the families who'd been coming for generations. Maybe it was beneath it all, the lessons, the technique, his belief that surfing was to do with how you thought about yourself, who you were. It was what he taught Ward from the beginning. The minute Ward could stand up and be held around the waist, balanced on his father's big board . . . And –

'Watch me, Wardy.'

That kind of command.

Over and over and over again.

'Copy me.'

Repeating.

'Be the same as me.'

'I want to be so proud of you.'

That stuff this morning, it's the same thing now as then. Being strong enough. Big enough. It's the way his dad is. The way he got talking early this morning about the water, some kind of wave that was going to come and might he be able to handle it . . . Ward looks out at the water and it's calm, and maybe hard to imagine it's going to mount up to anything, later on, but something . . . To do with the past still, maybe, the cold and where Ward's father's from, and the beaches around here having these currents, warm currents, and water that's so clear it's like turquoise sometimes, like . . . resort water, but this is no resort.

'You ready?'

Because what comes in with the warm sometimes is Ward's father's remembered cold.

It's what was going on this morning, for sure. This big northern wave that's got him so excited. How, certain days, and today is one of them, with the regular current you get also the seam of cold – it's what he always knew about, remember? Why he's always loved it here, for these strange rare days of tidal warm but the north comes in with new water, the cold from the place where he's come from.

Most people don't really know what Robert McFarlane's

talking about when he starts in about this. But Ward does. Though he's been too young to go himself, there've been maybe half a dozen times he can remember he's seen his father go out on this kind of a wave, in Spring, mostly, those Spring tides on his own and he'd catch them then, told Ward afterwards about the big swirling waves. How they were dark like in the ocean's belly as you caught them but then light to ride through and hard to stay in, always, hard to read . . . The warm and the cold. The cold and the warm. Big days. For Ward's dad, the best days. And going to come today, is what he said. 'A norther.' And how long now since the last one? One year? Two? Since Ward last saw his father out there on the water?

Something's going on.

Ward picks out his finger from the sand where he's been digging.

C-a-r-o-l-i-n-e.

His father, his mother, all that stuff this morning with them both . . . Ward could have brought the table down. Because, 'Watch yourself, little boy,' it's more like, no. Watch yourself, old man. Yourself. Because you're not even going into the water any more and where does somebody get off anyway, acting the way his father does? Doing the big thing with his mother now in front of him like they're the teenagers, he can't keep his hands off her. Baby, baby. And the stuff with the girls and not talking to Ward really, not really, starting out this morning like they were still buddies but that turning into a big fake the minute his mother came into the room.

It's fifteen.

Something about that, fifteen.

Like his father was once.

And Ward could ask his mother. What's going on? With his dad, all that? But he won't ask.

Fifteen, you don't do that stuff any more.

By then, fifteen, his father was a kind of a man.

ii

Ward's face burns, in the heat of this overhead sun
burn. He used to go to his mother all the time, ask her
anything, tell her anything. Like just to go to her and
ask what is it with his dad, what's going on . . . But so
he wants to, ask her? So? Only burn. This morning,
just remember, she stood by and let his father act that
way.

Ward looks out across the water. 'Don't hassle him,
Robbie' is all she said. 'What are you doing to him?'
They were still sitting there, the two of them, their feet
in a mess under the table and that way of looking at
each other . . . And just because his mother reached out
and took his hand, the feel of her cool hand holding his

62

hand while his father's eyes were on him, those blue, blue eyes . . . It wasn't like she could protect him. So why want to go to her, be with her like when she came down to the beach to be with him early this morning? So she said 'It's okay' after his father left the room, so her lips kissed the back of his hand when his father wasn't there to see . . . She may as well be the water. And look at this water. She's not going to tell him a thing.

Come on . . .

She only teases, murmurs love, comes creeping up to him on the sand.

Come on . . .

Like he could lose himself entirely in that sound, the sea's murmur, take his board out and stay. Not come back, have his father to deal with and those other kids to see. Not have Alex even, or that party, the girls, just nothing, nobody, only lose himself in sea . . .

And it's like the sea feels it too. She lets herself lie out flat beneath the burning sun, glisten, her surfaces blue and palm silver open to the day, little waves, barely moving. Like the boy she's inviting, *come on,* while the big tides start collecting inside her. Acting like all's gentleness here for her, but waiting, wanting one thing . . .

The sun shimmers through the air like a net he's trapped in, Ward closes his eyes.

Against the stillness of the air, the blue sky, the sea's like a sea seen from high above, looking down through the window of an aeroplane, so high you're miles and miles looking down to the surface like a rippled skin formed across the water, so thin you might draw your finger across and it would split open to the touch . . .

'Hey!'

He flicks opens his eyes.

'What are you doing?'

It's Alex. Standing right over Ward where he's sitting, his shadow on him.
    'Why are you still here?' he says.

Ward squints up, the light feels too bright suddenly, like he's been asleep, or dreaming. 'How long –' he starts to say.
    'Too long.' Alex grabs his hand, pulls him to his feet. 'Now come on!'

He's dressed, Ward can see. Long pants and a shirt that's not a T-shirt but it's fancy, a bit of it's come undone.

'I was thinking –'

Alex has started walking off. 'No thinking!' he says. 'We're late, they've been started since noon and we're still here, you're still here. I can't believe this . . .'

He's walking almost at a run now, Ward following.

'But I should go home first,' he says. 'Put something on.'

'There's no time for that . . .' Then Alex stops. 'Embarrassing for you, I know. When I'm looking so fine here, myself.' He does a little bow.

Up ahead is Beth's house, the last one along, and quiet looking but they're all inside, all the kids, and you can see, Alex . . . He wants to get there, now. He starts sort of half running again but then Ward says to him, 'You go ahead. I just need a minute,' and for the second time he stops.

'What did you just say?' Alex turns back to him. 'What I think you said? That you need a "minute"? Another "minute" for godsake? Jesus, Ward. You've just been here already for, like, forever. We're late you know. They started ages back . . .'

'I won't be long.'

'Yeah, yeah.'

Alex is mad, Ward sees the way he's squinting up his eyes and won't look at him. 'It's always "a minute" with you, Ward,' he's saying. 'It's always you just . . . Hanging around. Not joining in –'

'C'mon.' Ward steps towards him. 'C'mon.'

Alex is still looking away. 'I don't know . . .' but then Ward touches him, just on his shoulder, and Alex looks back at him then. For a second, this second, the two boys hold each other's eyes, on the beach, this day, this certain kind of light upon them, one in his shorts, the other with a fancy shirt and long pants on . . . Two boys . . . Then –

'Go,' Ward says.

And Alex does, he goes.

For the second time that day, Ward watches him run off down the beach, this time to just about where it turns, then he spins a left up through the bank and over the grass. He crosses the lawn in front of Beth's house, jumps up onto the porch, and disappears inside.

And suddenly . . . Emptiness. Is how it looks. Just the space on the beach where Alex was, a lonely passage down the sand. Ward sighs. This big dramatic sigh. Feels . . . What? Like a great gap open up within him? Like what's wrong with him anyhow that the slightest little normal thing, a party for godsake, makes him feel so apart from everyone else? Even Alex now? He looks up at Beth's and it seems like that house is somewhere he could never go. Though he's been there a million times before, this perfectly normal house, and he's promised, you know, he's promised . . .

It's so hot by now. The sand must be burning his feet. He's going to have to go back into the water. Before he can think anything more, about anything, just swim for a while, just breathe.

One stroke, two strokes . . .

The sand's still burning. He walks up to the edge of the sea, wades, dives . . .

And good.

To take a breath then, head under, have eyes wide open in the ocean again.

Good.

Again, to take a breath.

Good again.

And down.

The water slakes off him as he starts, a slow crawl, let the water bear him. Head down. Blowing out, arms over . . . Easy. Streaming, moving, head tilting to take a breath on the side, slice of air, slice of blue then under again . . .

Under . . .

And further.

Deeper.

After some time, he stops, treads. Looks around to see how far out he's come. It's a way. Beth's house, he can't even see it, the tide's pulled him around the point and he's out with the cliff the nearest, quarter mile. He tips his head back and with both hands pushes his hair right back from his face . . . That's nice. He's like an old man out here he's so familiar, like he's a bit of driftwood and his hair's a piece of weed. He goes under again. Eyes open. And the salt, the blue. Body of a boy maybe but it's like this water has always belonged to him, like he's been in this water forever.

Ward surfaces again, takes a breath. He turns over on his back and just floats, rests. It's been this way for him as long as he can remember. Being out this far in the ocean, this silence, and usually with his board . . . He was . . . Three? Four? When his father started pushing him over big waves and bringing him out to the deep? By five he was towing him out this far, anyhow, he remembers, that little piece of foam of his lashed to his dad's big fibreglass . . . They would come out together and okay, maybe they were gentle waves but big enough when you're five . . . Big enough. Lying on their stomachs on the beach after, like Sunday afternoon in the park only it wasn't, it was all their summers, and he was seven, he was eight, him and his dad hanging out together and by then he wasn't needing any kind of tow, he was doing it on his own, his dad with him maybe but paddling out on his own, moving his own weight through the water, the tired pull at the end of the day the thing Ward remembers most about those early summers . . .

'Make me proud, Wardy.'
   'Show me what you can do.'

Ward sighs thinking about it. And then there's Alex comes in, the two of them going out together, and the others too, and less and less with his father, but who chose that anyway? Whose decision that the father and son might stop being some kind of a team? By the time Ward was ten? Eleven? Getting his own main board, his father got him, that thing that must have looked like a freak to anyone who saw it, like a long board for a kid but some one had come shrunk it, and coming in on that . . .

'He was proud of me then, anyhow.'

The words jump out. Into the silence, the space of the ocean all around him.

'He was though.'

Coming in on that old cut-down board . . .

And Ward calling out to him, as his father rode alongside, 'Are you watching me, Dad? Are you watching me now?'

Man.

It lives.

How his father would say to him, 'You either understand your body or you don't. You have confidence in it, what it will do, or you don't.'

But now there's this silence around Ward's words and he's out here in the sea without his board, and his father . . . His father's nowhere near.

He should be heading back in.

Because he does have to go to this party, it's decided. Yeah, yeah. Ward knows.

If you let me, says the sea, *I'll give you the biggest time.*

He takes a breath, head under. Starts swimming in to shore.

iii

He gets back onto the beach again and the sun's like a mask. Ward blinks into it, and it does that thing again, the light, shadows, like oxidising into a kind of a print. What's the time by now? Must be three, easy, and . . .

The party.

Seems no avoiding it now. Ward dries down his arms, his chest. And what comes into my mind is this conversation he had a few days ago . . .

'Jenny and me, we're, you know . . .'
Some conversation with Alex.
'Don't tell me, man.'
A few days ago.

'I'm not interested,' Ward had said back to him, but Alex hadn't been able to let it go.

'We're together,' he'd said to Ward. 'Jenny and me. I want you to know about it.'

So . . . There's that. Another aspect of this afternoon, why Alex was pushing it, this whole party thing, pushing it, when they were out on the water before. And the dressed up attitude, the fancy shirt . . . Really, like Ward said to Alex before, he doesn't want to know a thing about it. Bad enough that it was behind all the stuff before, that talk when they were out, 'She likes you', probably, all that . . .

'It's great, it's better than you think –'

'Don't tell me.'

Bad enough.

'But I want to tell you. It's better than they say it is –'

Ward had turned away but still Alex had gone on and on, about him and Jenny together . . .

'Really.'

'Shut up!' Because really, you know. Does he want to have to think about this stuff? Imagine it? Like the dark nights you get this time of year, soft, and Alex and Jenny, they go to this special place in the dunes . . .

'Just shut up!' he'd said again.

72

But too late, because by then all of it was in. The words. The story. What's going on with the two of them stuck in his head . . . And he really, really doesn't want to go to this party. Like Ward and Alex won't be sitting round like they used to, you know, just be with each other, then leave . . . No. Now it's got to be talk, talk, talk and having to do some big act, kids lighting fires, making it down on the beach . . . A beer or two. Someone's got some grass, cool . . . It's all just . . .

Ward puts his hands to his ears like he might have put a shell there once.

. . . Too much.

Like he just wants things to be the same as before, I think so. Like when he was little he would put a shell to his ear this way. To close everything else out, the world, other people.

Hush.

The sound in the shell like the sound the sea makes, when you hold a shell to your ear. Only hear that sound, not Alex, not anybody. Only hush, that sound, the sound of the sea.

Hear it now?

Like a kind of silence for Ward? The sea? Like it allows
him to cast off from those other thoughts, complicated
thoughts, and the words . . .

Hush.

Let him think about nothing, maybe, or other, sim-
pler things . . .

The last time he was out, maybe. Yeah, think about that.
Was it last week? Before? Probably seems to Ward right
now that last time was forever ago. But remember how
good it was, the hush, hush sound now reminding him
maybe of the hush at the beginning then that turned
big. That was so good, a good day. Starting off clear,
then the water going cobalt in there, he'd been on his
own and it was nice . . .

Hush, hush . . .
Remember?

That sense of a slick coating the channel and just a frill
of wave to edge it, the tip of his board pointing through,
and a beautiful sense of the whole, deep water where he
was out in it but what lay below as well, the sand base
down there, stone and bits of rock and some bark even,
turned into something else by the salt, shell . . . Like

these fragments, resting below him with all this water, and him up and the board sweet, the frill of foam staying right there at his shoulder and the blue sky through the open end of the tunnel . . .

Remember?

Oh, yeah.
    That was it, a good day.
    Easy then, coming in, and long.
    Hold yourself up, then last minute crouch . . .
    Down, and . . . That's good. Hold it . . .

Ward can still make himself do this. For quietness. To hush the other stuff. More than parties, or Alex, he can make himself remember certain rides and go over and over them in his mind like other people might chant, maybe, or remember music, or say a poem or a prayer. For him he remembers things like the kind of splash around him as he was up, the quality of spray. The slick of the water beneath the board, he knows precisely how that felt, beneath the breast of the board, the tip, the kind of weight of the water beneath the sides. Or he can go over the glass of the channel in his mind, if it held or broke, estimating in seconds how long he stayed up, this ride or that one, he could clear it or not, make it last or not, or whether he knew from the outset he was only going to get a run at all before the wave would tilt him down . . . All stuff like this. Like that time last week . . . A good time, I think it was. Like I think it went turquoise for him as he hit midwater, going from dark to light, that feeling of the sea turning into air, a kind of buoyancy that takes you up and lets you stay, and when was it again? Friday? Only Friday? Seems much longer, like it always seems, like every time he's not out there he feels like he'll never get to do it again.

Remember? the sea's still whispering. Here with his hand against his ear.

The hush, hush?

Like a shell and all the sea in it. And what can any kid say, even Alex after all, compared to that? What can any party throw at him, any conversation, any talk, when he was out there, and he was deep . . .

Hush, hush.

The memory of the sea now, shifting on the shore, getting ready to move . . .

What is anything next to that?

Still, look what he's doing. Standing, burying down his board. Brushing sand off his legs, he'll go find his T-shirt in the dune. Up there is where it is, behind those grasses, okay put it on then, start making the walk to Beth's house, last one on the beach and not so far.

He heads up for the mid part of the beach where the sand's flattened down hard, where he and the others were standing around before, he goes past there, where it's wider. A few people have come back out on the beach by now, Ward's walking past them. Mr and Mrs Neilson, the Taylors. With their little kids, some others with them he's never seen. He keeps on walking.

'Hi there, Ward,' calls out Cole Taylor, he's out in the water with the littlest brother, showing him how to swim, looks like, with armbands and a miniboard.

'Hi.'

'Hi, Wardy!' The little kid shouting out. 'Look at me!'

'I'm looking.'

And he walks on, steps over a towel, someone's, there's a stripey bag with stuff in it, a book. It's like he sees all these things really vivid, like for the last time or some crazy thing . . . When he's only going to a party for godsake, a party, but he could sit down now, start talking to this woman here who's lying flat out with a magazine over her face, right now he's passing her, his foot practically by her face, he's never seen her before in his life, or the Edmonds guy beside her, the Edmonds kids building a sandcastle down by the water . . . Any of them. He could hang out with any of them, spend time, easier, with someone he doesn't even know, rather than walk on to this party now . . . But still . . . He keeps . . . Walking. Getting. Closer.

And the music, from Beth's house, he can hear it from here, what's playing, some old seventies thing, like . . . He can't even think what it might be. More like a beat he can hear, it's the beat he's hearing, not the tune, and that girl . . . Yeah, sure, she'll be there, but that was probably some mistake anyhow, her touching his arm before, that would have been just . . . Nothing. Alex saying all that stuff before, humming dumb Costello . . . Even so, Ward makes himself keep walking, over the old buffalo grass lawn now, past Beth's kid brother's bike, a little kid board, a pile of goggles, flippers, stuff . . . Past the little band of flowers growing up by the porch, jumping up on the porch and pushing open the swing door.

It's dark inside. Ward's eyes take a second to adjust to the suddenness of it, after the bright glare of being outside to come into this, and he walks deeper in, to the sitting room, and then it's like all he sees through the darkness is girls. They're sitting around with their swimsuits on, lounged on Beth's parents' sofas and chairs, the curtains drawn against the day. A couple of them are smoking, or stretched out on a sofa, lounged back, legs over each other like half asleep, the whole thing some kind of picture.

Ward just stands there. It is like a picture, girls sitting around in the half dark. And of course the guys are there, Ward can see them now too, standing up by the walls and talking a bit, the music's on but it's not that loud. Everyone looks exhausted, like Ward's come upon them here, this kind of a tableau, an underwater scene. Jenny's head's back against the back of the sofa, her eyes closed like she's sleeping but then she calls out 'Hey, Ward', and a couple of others look over, go, 'Hey', 'Hey'.

It's as though everything is happening in slow motion. Second by second here. Beth comes over to Ward now, with a glass, and she presses it cold on his shoulder.

'I made some margaritas,' she says. She passes it to him, the glass, which is full of a kind of pale lime colour.

'Thanks.'

And slowly, it seems, he takes it from her.

She watches him take the first sip. And the second.

'You like it?'

'Yeah.'

The glass has salt. Ward takes another sip.

'Yeah?'

'Yeah.'

Still, it looks weird around him. Like the kids here, they were all outside before and they all know each other pretty well but now . . . Everyone lying around, this kind of stillness . . . It's like they're completely different.

Though Ward's been in this house a million times, been invited, sat around with Beth's parents in this same room, it's all different, really it is, like a picture he's come in on, some kind of play or film and everyone has a part to play but he doesn't know who he's supposed to be, nobody told him.

Sarah comes up to him then, that moment as he takes another sip from his glass, and she smiles, 'Hey, Ward . . .'

Her hair's pushed back from her face with her sunglasses and she has this red swimsuit on.

She says, 'Glad you came. Alex said you would.'

And . . . You know. It's just Sarah. She was wearing that same swimsuit before.

'Well,' Ward says. 'I had a swim. I guess . . .'

'You got delayed,' she says.

'Exactly, that's it. I got delayed, I –'

'Doesn't matter, Ward. I'm not accusing you!'

She laughs then, a kind of a strange, tinkly kind of laugh, and there's that weird feeling again, like everything's gone into stillness here, like Sarah's face in front of Ward's face, her laughing, is different from anything he's ever seen in her and it's fixed, in time, set in this second, this particular kind of strange laugh, but then that second breaks and she carries on talking, like easy, like always, this party the most normal thing in the world and all the kids here together and this darkened room, this is normal, everyone lying around, stretched out all over the Levers' fancy sofas and chairs.

Ward finishes what's in his glass, goes over to the table where the bottles are, pitchers of the same pale green coloured drink. He refills his glass, standing there at the table, takes a sip straight away and another. Beth's come over with him and now he sees Jenny get up from the sofa, a girl Ward doesn't know reaching out her arm to stop her, but she comes over anyway. She sneaks up behind Beth and puts her hands over Beth's eyes.

'Monkey see nothing,' she says, then she takes her hands away. 'Hi, honey,' she says. She kisses Beth on the side of her face. 'Everyone's here.'

She puts her arms around Beth's waist, and Beth's arm is around her waist. They look at each other, and smile.

'Hi, honey, to you,' Beth says.

Then Jenny says to him, 'Hi Ward. You made it.'

All he can do is nod. He's standing right here next to these two and he's rigid, somehow. Like it's not ever going to be possible for him to move. There's Beth's hand around Jenny's naked waist, Jenny's around Beth's . . .

'You seen Alex?' Jenny says to him now. 'How dressed up he is?' She points over to the corner where Ward sees Alex for the first time, still wearing his grown-up shirt but unbuttoned all the way through by now, right down the front. Ward sees him tilting his head back to finish the last of what's in his glass, then he shakes his head, mouths the word 'wow!'

Jenny keeps her finger pointed there towards him. Maybe she's drunk. Maybe everyone is. There's the smell of green too, maybe she's high.

'Isn't this fun?' Beth says. 'My parents are away for . . . Two. Whole. Days.'

Ward has some more of his drink, finishes it. Maybe everyone is drunk here. Alex in his long pants and undone shirt, the girls in their suits . . . He sees Jenny take her arm away from Beth and all of it seems slow, slow, like maybe they all are drunk here and he sees Jenny go over to Alex, come up from behind, and she wraps both her arms around his waist and Alex turns and they start to kiss.

Yeah, well. Ward might want to close his eyes if he could, at this point, not to have to see this. I don't think he wants to see. But that would just be too weird. The idea that he couldn't bear to see his best friend like this, be part of it, don't you think? His best friend in the world getting off with this girl? To close his eyes would be weird, it's true, but you know it's weird to be looking at them too. Like his parents, when his parents act up that way, how he feels then's like now, that there's no part of him wants anything to do with any of this, when this kind of stuff happens, and it's happening now, people pairing off, two by two, two by two . . .

Ward turns away, swipes another drink off the table. They do taste okay. His mother makes margaritas sometimes, same thing.

'Aren't they the best?' Sarah says. 'You know she made them, like, not from a mix.'

'She me,' Beth says, she laughs.

It's another one of those strange laughs, but . . . Maybe it's not so bad. You know? To be here? Like he thought this morning, when he came out from hiding in the trees . . . They're his friends, after all. So some people are off kind of doing it, not everyone is, these girls are here, Sarah's here, Beth's here. Ward chinks his glass against theirs.

'Thanks for inviting me,' he says.

'It's fun,' Sarah says.

'Yeah.' Ward waits a second, then says, 'I mean, I suppose. I mean. Did you make these?' he says to Beth.

'I just said –' she says and she's smiling. Then she shakes her head. 'I don't know, Ward. You're so . . . Weird. None of us get to see you, really, do we? You don't usually come to any of our things, and we do lots of little things, don't we girls?'

She takes a sip from her drink. She looks hard at

Ward, up and down. 'Even here,' she says, 'at the beach even, no one really gets to see you, you're so quiet. And that board of yours. Do you think it's normal, Ward?'

Someone laughs, Sarah.

'No seriously. I'm being serious here. Do you think it's normal to avoid us? Do you? What does your dad say about it?'

'Yeah, your dad,' says Sarah. 'You're dad's so cool.'

'Does he think you should, like, get out more?' Beth sips at her drink again. 'I think your dad's great, actually. Isn't he?' She turns now to someone else who's just come up. 'Ward's father?' she says. 'He must have been so, like, you know,' Beth says. 'When he was young.'

'He still is,' Jenny says. She's come back over to join them. 'I think.'

Beth says to her, 'You're right,' and they both laugh.

'Oh, Ward,' Jenny says. 'Poor you.' She takes another sip, looking at Ward, only at him now, over the rim of her glass.

'But you know,' she says then. 'We're all cool, right? Not just Ward's dad,' and then she reaches out, she makes a kind of a little hook with her finger, and she catches one of Ward's fingers that way. Holds onto it. She's smiling at him, taking another sip from her drink. She's saying 'Yeah', and her teeth are very white against her tan, and the whites of her eyes, in this darkened room with the light outside those covered windows, where the sky is, the sea is, glittering, restless . . .

'Yeah,' she says again.

Ward doesn't move, just his little finger, caught in hers . . . Out there, beyond the window with its curtains is the sea, and yes the sea is waiting but starting to turn . . .

. . . Movement in the channel, fresh swell, the tide . . .

But still Ward can't move. He does have to close his eyes. The drink hitting. This girl getting close. There's the feeling of her face, her body, like the air is getting closer, warmer and something in the air, like a strength, a kind of power that's about to break through, push open the space between now and when something's going to give. Like a wave, before the break. Holding for a second, a second and then . . .

The big slide, the big dip.

'Whoa,' says Jenny, and she's right up against Ward now. And she's doing something, with her other hand she's playing with his hair, putting little bits of it back behind his ears. 'Easy,' she says, as he can't help but lean in. 'Surfer-boy,' she says, and then the pressure of her lips are against his lips, and it's just an instant but they're together like that, the press of their mouths against each other and she softens against him, her lips opening and a feeling of a slide and . . . It explodes, for Ward, of that second of her tongue in him, now they're kissing and he starts to move, him and this girl together and it's like everything is split open, come undone at the joinings, everything, the shock and now the wave, he's no longer standing, he's free-fall, not here, not anywhere . . .

Is what it's like.

Is like.

Then Jenny breaks from him.

'See?'

She smiles up at him. She's standing right there in front of him in her bikini. 'It's fun, right? It's not hard at all . . .'

There's a kind of laugh behind her, and now Ward can see a whole bunch of them, all these girls, sitting on the sofa behind her, they've seen the whole thing.

'Looked fun to me,' says one of them, and then Alex yells out, 'Hey! I saw that! And she's supposed to be my girlfriend!' and laughs, everyone laughs.

Ward stands, as though he feels the kiss in him and can't move from it, drunk, the people here, Alex, pretty girls. Everywhere he looks, pretty girls. In this dark room, sitting, touching, kissing. Girls with damp hair and swimsuits, their legs around the legs of boys, their arms twining around . . . Jess and Beth and Jenny and Pamela and Kate . . . Ward knows all their names, all the girls in this room, sitting here in Beth's parents' house in the dark while Beth's parents are out, kissing and letting boys touch them on Beth's parents' sofas and chairs . . .

Yeah.

Taking off their swimsuits, unpeeling the salty cloth . . . Slowly and deliberately, in Beth's parents' bedroom, maybe, by her parents' big bed, undoing the straps from their bikinis, pulling the tops of their swimsuits down so they can see themselves in the big mirror, dark from the sun where the sun has got to them and white like animals in the other parts . . .

All the girls . . .

And see? says the sea, outside the window, beyond the curtain's cloth.
   What I can do, who I am?
   See? As the girls unpeel themselves slow?
   Melt and burn and turn, do you see? How they're like me?

And just that moment Ward notices the other girl, Alison, she's over by the window on her own. She smiles. She leans back against the wall. And they're all drunk here, Ward's drunk. He tries to smile back at her but someone's pulling his hair from behind.

'Wardy. Hey, Wardy.'

And all he can do is let his head go back, like lying out on the water and the sea, she holds him up.

Noon

The sea has . . .

Contemplation, gets to see stuff, watch
one boy,

wrist cords dangling in the water, orange, fluorescent
green, flicking water at the other who lies quite still, his
arms down at his sides, plunged to the elbow in sea.

And perfect flat that surface is, like all the time in the
world is here and never going to change from noon, from
now, the past the present, and the present the past . . .

One boy,
two boys . . .

A father,
or his son . . .

It's all the same for this sea.

She lies now beneath the boards, very still. It's noon and the sun's eye is upon her but even the old sun can't see what's inside, deep in the dark waters. All my secrets, says the sea, and she wants more, she wants to keep all the boys. She feels the shift within her when there's a touch of even one of them upon her skin. The one with wristlets dangling, or the one whose slim weight she feels upon her back . . .

One.
  Two.

Her tides are getting ready to have them, like the muscles of currents opening, relaxing, contracting . . . Getting ready to move her surfaces open, to form ripples, waves . . .

Two boys.
  One . . .
  Two . . .
  And whether it's now, or later . . . .
  Makes no difference, time, to this water.

The woman on the shore looks out, shades her eyes against the glare, but she can't see her son or his friend any longer, like she used to lose sight of her husband too, when he took their boy out that far. They've drifted away past the point so she goes back to the house where it's cool, lies down there in a room alone, closes her eyes . . .

All my secrets . . .

She feels herself drift, change, into sleep, her tides taking her . . .

'Come on' . . .
    And there's her son now, far out, in her dreams he's drifting away . . .
    A little deeper, the sea says.
    It's cool here, it's nice . . .

'But I don't want to!'

And the sea, she gets to see stuff, remember . . .
The one uncertain on his board, the other up and riding . . . 'Come on, now! Don't be a baby!'

The woman starting in her sleep: 'I love you two!'

Because one boy, two boys . . .
    Father or son . . .
    To the sea they're all the same.

Mine . . .

She opens her mouth and all the boys slide in.

THREE

i

Suddenly there's this feeling of how late it is. Like Ward must have passed out or something and he can't even see outside with these curtains closed, what the weather's doing, it must be late into the afternoon by now . . . But no. But yes. It's late.

He gets up, steps over empty glasses and a bottle or two. There's stuff all over the floor, ashtrays, cushions. Some music's on, some kids are dancing, but the room seems empty, and something must have happened. To put him so out of it, asleep or whatever, some joint going around, could have been . . .

Either way: Get out of here. He heads straight down the

hallway, pushes open the swing door and the heat hits him, the light, like a wall. After all that darkness, this wide hot air and –

Ward stops.

That's a twenty.

A thirty even.

The wave come right up just like he thought. There it is, in front of him, the pull in the centre and holding, like a carved wave, blue glass, a mountain. Clean from the north and high like just like his dad said . . . Ward starts running. Back to the sea, across the beach for his board where he left it and sure he could use something bigger but no way there's time. Every second the sea's forming, closing in. Why for a minute even did he think he could be away? From this? Yellow sun, sand like a slick of black paint and the blue, blue ocean . . . Why be inside ever when out here there's this, all this? So he keeps running, faster, bits of sand flicking up at him as he runs and it's only when he sees not just the shape of the whole water but someone out there on it, a board, that he stops, suddenly, like he's been hit, someone out there before him . . . Alex.

Except it's not Alex. Wrong colour. His orange board . . .
You'd see Alex anywhere with his colour and this guy's
far out, whoever he is, the colour of his board hard to
see. Ward shields his eyes. No. He can't see. The water's
carrying the guy though, he looks good out there, his
arms straight out and coming in perfect, holding it,
holding it, a little figure set as though motionless against
the blue glass mountain at his back. Just look at him go.
Because sure you don't get water like this every day, like
it's the first day of the world or something, the way it
seems to be creating itself before Ward's eyes . . .

He starts running again, gets up onto the dune where
the two boards are parked, Alex's orange, his own green
and blue. He never did do that re-fixing, or put on the
wax . . . Too late now. He pulls out the length and is
down to the water. Starts out, pushing off and paddling
. . . And immediately it feels . . .

Mighty in here.

Like he's only gone out a few strokes but already there's
the tug of the in-come and it's going to be some work
getting himself out to the break, but worth it, this is,
today is. He puts his head down so his arms can really
push through, to find a path would be good, like the
other guy must have found a rip to get him out that far

99

. . . Ward looks up to see him. There he is, coming in through the tunnel and the pitch he's holding, like he's sited himself precisely, to the side, hips weighted low against the wave edge and arms out but only a little way, all the balance from within . . .

It's his dad.

Of course. Is how things were always going to go here, isn't that right? That it would be his father here before him. That the man who's kept himself apart from the water all this time would choose this moment, this afternoon, to come back in. It's what the day's been about, where it's been leading, the sense of shape to a story like the shape of a wave made from intersecting tides . . . That after how many months, years? Two years? Of course it's him out there. From the talk before, the morning . . . 'You going?' to Ward being inside with the girls, him inside while his dad was out back in his shed, polishing down his old nine-liner and getting ready, for this . . .

Look at him.

The pitch of his ride, the slow right, the flick of white at the top, the break all around him but himself not breaking . . . It's like no one else. All the way coming in and no crouch on the board, just standing there . . . No one else is like that, no one. Ward can't make himself stop looking . . . After all this time, to see his father back up and coming in . . .

Of course he can't stop looking. A kind of breathlessness in him, I think, no, breath*fullness* is what it is. Like everything inside him has grown suddenly, is enlarged by feeling, like the heart is, the ribcage expanded to hold it, like the volume of breath inside him's too big for his body. And look at him. Look at him still . . .

The ride continues as Ward just has to stay, watching. The sea pulling him out but not to where he should be yet all he can do is keep watching his father. Cutting back, coming in again, in and back, over and over like an angel, the endless repetitions seeming to hold in time, in motion, as though eternal, and then, though it seems impossible, start to fold, diminish, the wave completing in on itself and his father turning in. Ward sees him complete, get up, then start straight away the long paddle out again.

'Dad!' He calls out, loud as he can against the swell but by now, of course, that man's too far away. Ward may want to join him, but they're far apart, the tide pulled Ward eastwards while his father's direction's to the south-west.

'Dad!' Ward calls again, starts paddling hard to where his father is, to get out there himself, it's all he can try to do, 'Dad! Let me come out with you!' Because he has to, he's never been in this height of water before and he needs his father here and make the sea help him, get him there: Like, come on . . . and –

Okay, says the sea, and she pulls suddenly at his board but not across but out this time, to help his paddle, to catch a current . . . Okay? Okay. So this way, still following his father's progress with his eyes, Ward tries to keep in course, and feeling now this nice pull, the change. Better. Moving now, working, and *come on*, says the sea, and, okay, okay, further out, and out, and if the sea has her way, keeps moving him this direction, their paths should cross but if Ward's father's noticed he hasn't acknowledged. The board surges forward again, catches, takes Ward out again in a sweep with little effort . . . Out he goes, out and out . . .

And the view's like the movies. Where he is now, five out and easy and the shimmer of light on the water and his father getting closer and closer . . . The boy to the man . . . The man to the boy . . . Two boys . . .

'Hey!' Ward calls out, but still nothing comes back. No answer, no wave.

'Hey!' Ward calls again, but the other one just continues moving himself powerfully through the water like nothing is against him, like nothing could ever be against him, while for Ward there's this surge of the tide rising up below for an answer, *Mine!*, as the sea takes him all the while further out, and further, the water like great whales of water riding up before him now, rising up and diving . . . And for the first time Ward registers, as the tug wants to pull his board out to the side and down and it's all he can do to stay on, how huge, really, how huge this water is.

From shore . . . You couldn't see from back there, not really. Couldn't notice fully the actual size of the tips, the way the pull was coming in so strong. But now, suddenly, it's like there's a kind of a sense of depth here to each wave that's nothing he's ever known before, like the height of the wave is holding its own water weight in depth to match it, the gravity going two ways. Ward felt it when he first came into the water, remember? That feeling of a pull and a push at the same time but then there was the thing of his father and seeing him and not noticing water exactly then only –

Now . . .

Ward's seeing it around him in hills. Like coming in

103

mountains these blue sides of water and no sense of how they'll fall or rise they're just on you, come for you around on all sides, like a giant room of sea and the board has to find a way out of it, somehow, to pitch over, get past. That surfing is your body, sure, like his father's always said, but this . . . How to use your body in this . . . The sea's the only body.

Ward feels himself slip across again on the next pull, trying still to keep his father's progress in sight, but a new swell comes up behind obscuring him and all Ward can see then is motion, a spiralling in, like a giant plug of water sucking in his board and taking him straight down, for a second or two, before he can come up again and right himself, there's just this washing over him of blue, blue-green and salt and . . . Pale, like water he's never seen, what it is, he doesn't really know what to do with it. He re-settles himself with more weight to the back, to let the board be more taken, but . . . There again . . . It is . . . That kind of a sideways charge it had just then, with that last surge, like with two currents in it, when he was down, he felt the two, and the colour, that colour . . . Like resort water only this is no resort – and then the thought slides whole into his mind: The warm and the cold. It's that.

Don't think about that now.

But it is. Everything about being out here. What his father's always talked about but Ward's never been inside it until now . . . The warm and the cold, those two tides together like the sea's formed from a different kind of temperature and nothing to do with current patterns or some wind come in . . .

Don't think about it.

And actually, you know what? You can't. Right now. Think. You can't choose anything at all about this water . . .

Only come,
  further out, where the other one is.

Because it's sea here and there's nothing else . . .
  Out and further, down.
  Two boys, and what the sea's doing, what the sea's going to do to them.

Ward feels that power as he slips out, further, with his father. Out and down, *cool darkness,* where long silver fish slide in and out of the crevices, between the seams of tide . . . *Deeper, colder* . . . The shining blue water carrying him like shining, dissolving, into giant melt down there, somewhere way below him, past miles and miles of this pale salt that stings his eyes into endless, eyeless dark . . .

And the sound starting now.

Boom.

From deep in. The lovely warm and the cold.

Boom.

Hundreds of tonnes of water compacting, exploding.

Boom.

The sound all around the boy like the beat of his enlarged heart.

Boom.
　Boom.
　Boom.

So you can forget all about 'I don't want to!' There is no choice. Ward doesn't have a choice, is why he's here, how he was raised. You going? He's never had that choice, not really. Like never a choice not to watch when his father said 'watch', make him proud when his father said 'make

me proud'. It's terrifying here, amazing, this splendid
terror of the water, but don't say this is about heroism,
him choosing to be here like his father chose . . .

Boom.

'No!'

Because there is no choice.

He may call out now, 'I don't want to!' but the reply
comes back:
  'Don't worry!'
  'But I'm scared!'
  'There's nothing to be scared of!'
  And the sea going, *come on.*
  'I don't want to!'
  Make him want to.
  Smiling, pretending.
  'You know you want to.'
  'I don't want to!'
  'Don't be a baby, Wardy. Show me what you can do.'

So it's all come together, in these same tides come. Out
here alone with his father Ward knows, it's in the size of
his heart: Boom. Two currents, the warm and the cold.
I don't want to. 'Course you want to.

Boom.

And all he can see is water by now. The side of the next wave approaching.

Boom.

And his father beyond him, up on his board and yelling over to him now, this big grin on his face, in the centre of a huge ocean and the wave that's about to take him . . . Yelling, 'Isn't this great?' over the water.

Boom.

'Get up!' He gestures, catches.

Boom.

'Ride in with me!'

Boom.

'There's nothing at all to be afraid of here!'

ii

And there isn't. For the man on the board it seems there's nothing to be afraid of, like it's a moment of pure memory this, being out and huge water but he's controlling it, someone there to watch him come in . . .

Is how it looks. As though he knows, this man, what to do, how to be. How, riding easy to start out with, you keep yourself up like he keeps himself up now, and high. And the feel of his body, its dimension, against the pressure of this particular water . . . That's something he does know plenty about, remember, like something he can read as though it were a set of numbers maybe, some pieces of a sign. There's the splay of his foot, this man's foot a certain kind of shape, kept neat along the left edge, five toes working like a grip and keep them there, that's a little line up, good, and his right foot out maybe 45 behind. That's it, looking fine. Weighted back at the heel, about two feet behind's a good distance for this size of wave, and keep the body evenly distributed through the arms, into the hips. And –

Hold it.

Perfect. Arms . . . Okay, they can play a little now, but elbows into the side, palms flat, what was that thing his old daddy used to call them, like a couple of spatulas . . . That was it.

And flip back. Weight again to the back. His old daddy. Long time ago it was when that old man used to watch him . . . And what became of him anyhow? While he makes the weight to the left, holds it, drops the knees . . . Didn't he just let that old man . . .

Go.

Yeah. Ward's father rights himself. He did, though. Long time ago . . . Let his father loose into the past. And sure that was beautiful just then when he could have lost it but didn't, held it right over the edge. Kept his posture exact, not moving a part of him to change a thing, just staying, while the push of the wave is under there, right there at the top third of the board . . . And maybe he shouldn't have, you know . . . Gone so far away, the way he did, from his own father, left him so far behind . . .

But, this.

Oh, this is . . .

Endless now. Like endless tunnel here and nothing can stop him. Not the past, an old man. Thinking about him now . . . Talking about him . . . Because wasn't he, anyhow . . . Crazy?

Ward's father holds it, holds it.

Had to be.

Makes it slightly to the right, comes back centre again.

Living by himself up there, way out to sea with those boards he made . . . He had to be crazy, didn't he? The old man? Like this ride is, had to be?

But . . .

Beautiful.

This is. This man feels himself turn now, slightly to the left, just the upper torso the turn and . . . Keep holding it . . . Hold it . . . Just then, making that turn to the left, holding it . . . It's the warm and the cold. That big kind of sea like you got up there then, in those days when he was a boy living up north alone with his father . . .

He angles back again now. Back into the same move from before, shoulders square on, the curl on his left. At his side, tunnelling, forming, the cold, and it's the warm coursing through that lifts the wave, two kinds of water here, this water, it's beautiful, crazy. And that old man, a son to raise . . .

Easy, easy.

Living way up there all by himself . . .

He pitches forwards slightly, to catch himself right on a tug, steadying back again to keep the tube . . .

And he's never been back to see him . . .

He breathes in deep, holds.

Never. This man on the board. Who was a boy once, who saw how carefully his father gathered shells, pieces of wood off his beloved shore. 'The gentlest man I ever knew.' Who said that? His mother?

The man on the board doesn't even know his mother's name.

Breathing in, breathing out. Keeping his arms at his sides.

He doesn't remember his mother's face. Or her voice, or touch.

And there's no way, anyhow . . . Is there? That he could have stayed? Growing up there, on that remote part of the coast, dangerous water and that cold, needing more than one father could give, no way?

And yet . . .

There's this breadth now beneath him as he rides off the water and it seems to me here, looking on here, like it's some kind of a reminder, of something from back then, the world he left all that time ago, of her, his mother, the water . . . And his father taught him that, didn't he? That she would hold him, like all of us can be held? That she

would always hold him. And the writing and the paint-
ing and the things that old man made, the way that old
man himself went out into the water . . . He gave the
sea to his boy this way. When there was so much he
couldn't give, he taught him: Control the things you
understand, don't think about the other part. Like too
much sea there'll always be more out there trying to
devour you if it can, but those big waves that used to
crash on the beach at night, remember? They never did
come in, did they? So maybe not so crazy after all, old
man, maybe, and where are you now anyway, still up
there? Still waiting for the perfect wave to take you? I
bet. And old by now, so old, and this man here on the
board, he's getting older too. Money on the screen, okay,
a wife, a child, but there's some cold coming in off the
northern ocean and the tug of the warm tide running
through and . . . That gift you gave him's been turned
into something he's tried to own, not let himself be held
by so all he wants to do now is keep himself on the surface and ride, only ride . . .

The sea picks Ward's father up, takes him on, in. The
mighty tunnel at his back ever forming. Makes this
beauty swell beneath him, and in the end he's a man
here and a boy, and both the sea has always known. The
kind of kid who'd abandon, be abandoned. Who never
went back to see his father, who's all sinew that way,

resolving things that happened into bone and muscle within his body, but not his heart.

All he sees is himself. The wave catches, rolls. He doesn't see his son who's getting closer towards him, paddling towards him . . . Coming up alongside . . . Hair in ropes down his back like in plaits and tied with rags, just a kid but on a mighty board, and getting up now, this second, bit by bit, using the strength of his young arms to take his weight, bring his back leg forward to steady himself, steady . . .

And the sea has them both, this minute.

One.
   Two.

And she rises up, gets ready.

Ward brings his leg forward a bit more, to weight himself, support himself, there he is, and you see what's going to happen, can't change it, the thunderous motion of the water . . .

Boom.

Louder, now he's getting up, than when he was paddling, the sea sounds, and Ward brings forward his other leg now . . . To crouch . . . Stand . . . He's never known water like this, the channel headed straight for him and his father coming though, the sea here, the sea, with no chances, she contains him . . . The sea, the sea . . .

And time . . .

Makes no difference, time, to this water. Ward's up and riding now, look at him, standing up alongside his father, coming in . . . Like all the sea's afternoons is here, the sun stopped in its dusty path, time turned back to gold. Afternoon of this one day but all time in it, sun stopped high overhead, dust of heat in the air like the gauze of harvest, sacrifice, gold coming down off the sides of the sky from the court of gold . . .

Watch me!

One boy, up on his board.

Watch me!

Like he used to call to his father, like his father to his father also called. And this long waited for water, for hours, days, predicted by the weather, by night's stars, arrived at last, come in from somewhere as though from another world. That's what Ward thought, isn't it, isn't that what I wrote before? Like from some new part of the world's water was what Ward was seeing, when he first came outside this afternoon? Now he's up and coming in, fully up now behind his father, up there just the same on this water, this size of water he's never been on, as though it's formed of all the waves, all the rivers, oceans, seas . . . All the summers, all the suns that have ever held high and true in the sky, all the days' suns, is in the heat that falls on the boy's back . . . Time, that beats a drum in his heart, that plays in his hair so though it's tied with rag it's cornsilk, gold . . .

'Watch me, Dad!'

And . . .

'Can you see me?'

And that minute, second, the sea comes up behind, catches the flick of the rags in his hair, and she opens up the channel to take him . . .

Boom.

But no.

It's his father goes down instead.

Ward sees it happen, tips round, steadies himself as the roar he hears in the water passes on to get his father's board, not his board.

Boom.

It was his father the sea wanted all the time. Ward crouches down, using the board beneath him for ballast but the tug is enormous, pulls him down . . . He's under the water now, but up again, and coming up he pushes, harder, he has to, using all his strength to get over, to get even close to where he saw his father go over.

Boom.

His father's nowhere to be seen. Ward can't even see his father's board. Only the next heave of water rising up and over –

Boom.

'Dad!'
  Suddenly there doesn't seem near enough time.
  'Dad!' He calls out but though he's close he's not close enough because his father's down there somewhere,

underneath all that water, and he's not close enough and not time enough now that time's started up again . . .

And Ward's under again. Swallowing water, lost footing, the boom gone. The swirl of the board up there some- where through the water then his head's pulled down further, and there's nothing but water, the sea's charge, Ward being pulled down, further, down, his legs up are up above him somewhere, but his body's spiralling, turning over . . . *Mine, mine* . . . Then he sees the board, the green, the white, catches it, spinning, comes up, and there's air. He's gulping air. Then he smashes it under him again, the board, to balance again, it's back under his body again and he's up again, he's up, it's okay . . .

But madness. To have followed his father here, madness, and where is his father now . . .

He emerges that second, just an arm, then his head. For a second Ward sees his father's face, sees him take a mighty gasp of air and the water closes over him again. Ward uses the left side of himself to keep back from that part of the wave base but there's a pull, deep down, is sucking right down now, like a plug being pulled to the middle of the earth, pulling, taking Ward's father way down there . . .

Ward lunges again, to catch him. Slips his own board, but manages to half hold while the side of the water before him's like thick glass and for another second he sees his father's body there behind it like behind a window and . . . Ward dives then, into the glass. The leg-rope goes taut, then the board hits out hard against the side of the water, it's like all he did was bounce against the surface. His father's gone.

His board flips up onto the surface alone and no part of his father to see now, not his dark head, an arm extended. Ward tries again against the part he went into before, into the side of the wave, using his arms to chop against it. Just to get back to that second ago, to get the sea to take him there, great mouthfuls of air, to that part where he just saw his father trapped in. He keeps . . . Pushing. Towards . . . That part. Though the sea. Keeps . . . Pushing. But then . . . How it happens. How Ward manages to reach out, break through the water into a piece of the wave and there's the older man's arm, how his hand manages to grab hold of that arm . . .

And here . . . Emerging, coming out of the water, his head breaking through the glass surface . . . Ward never to this day knows how it happened, how he could pull this man out of that water so that he can get his hand now, grab his father's hand and pull, pull . . . Never knows. And how his father feels, his face shocked by water, by the pain of staying alive in this water, keeping enough breath in him to keep himself alive in this water . . . Ward never knows how he did it, could get his hand to break through the glass. Grab his father's arm, then hand, bring his father's body up, so that his father is held up now by his son, lifted through the water, through the broken water that's all around them in great pieces . . . And –

'Keep hold of me, Dad.'

The danger of the wave itself has passed.

Moved on, smiling. One board gone, Ward pulls his father up onto his own and only the swell left. Ward's father taking great gulps of air, retching, water and vomit heaved from him . . . Resting on his son's board against his son who's pushing him through the water, Ward pulling him all the way, the weight of him all the way . . . Back onto the beach, far enough down near Falcon's after all, and there, before anyone else can come up upon them, this is what he turns to Ward now and says:

'Well that was fun. You ready to go out again?'

With the spit still coming out of him, the puke, and this big gash from where the board got him at the side, and trying to grin, he looks at his son. 'You ready? To go out there again?' Wincing in pain, you know, but still saying it, saying it. 'Back you go, boy. Don't you know how proud I was of you out there?'

And Ward . . . Ward looks back at him.

His father's lifted his two fingers to point at him, as the two of them are still gasping here for breath, and Ward can hear the voices of everyone coming down upon them now, coming down here where they are on the beach, going 'You okay? You okay?', still here's his father looking up at him, these two fingers of his pointing at Ward like a little gun, saying 'How does it feel? To make your old dad so proud?'

And Ward slowly shakes his head, no.

Looking back at his father, not saying anything, and that man, pointing his fingers of a gun towards his son, turns those same fingers back to his own temple then and fires.

Boom.

His mouth mimes the word. Then he closes his eyes.

iii

There's a crowd gathered around them on the beach. There's Alex, some of the kids, the girl who's been around, Alison . . . And other people, who've been watching from shore or come outside from their houses. Ward himself can't speak. Richard's dad has made his father lie out along the sand and his leg – 'Don't move him at all,' Richard's dad says – is broken. Clean, someone said, and then there's the blood all the way down the side of him but he's going to be alright, someone said that too.

'Make some room, don't come too close.'
    Like there's objectivity here, Ward will think later.
    'Jesus, I saw the whole thing.'

That this is an accident, but that's all it is. It's not a tragedy. There's been a mistake, some kind of misunderstanding, but now let's call the doctor, sort it out. Everything's, you know, going to be okay.

'Don't talk about it,' someone says.

'Yeah, but did you see them out there?'

'The water –'

'The sea.'

'I mean, who would go out in that . . .'

'Only these two . . .'

'Oh, boy . . .'

' Would have to be these two alright.'

Sure there's no strength left in Ward's father, little in Ward's body by now, the impact of what he's done, pulling them both in, the full weight of another person and trawling that on a board, compacting . . . But enough strength too. That he could still support his father the last couple of yards up out of the water, just lose the board and have him by then in his arms, lay him down in the sand. Then someone, Richard's dad it was, and some other guy, were there and they took over then, checked his father's pulse, his breathing, and there's a cut, blood. Already it's congealing, set by the sea like running wax gone hard, wet and clear still in some places, this vividness Ward can see on his father's long body, this wild opening in his skin. Someone says his name, 'Ward!' but he can't look up, even for a second from where he's kneeling, to see who was that, a friend, any of the kids who've come looking, there's too much weakness in his father for Ward to bring his head up now and look them in the eye.

'You did some thing, Ward.'

He only wants to stay beside his father here.

'You did.'

And there are these voices.

'Somebody's called emergency services.'

'An ambulance, someone's coming in a car . . .'

More voices.

'It's coming . . .'

And the sense of the crowd ebbing and flowing around him, the late afternoon, but all Ward can do, it seems, is kneel here, while time is passing and the ambulance comes, and a stretcher, an injection, more talking, and then his father is taken away.

The sun is slowly going down. Not cool exactly but something low in the air like a great shadow forming and the crowd disperses, the sea like a silver engine turned off. It's so quiet now, and all the water's calm, like none of the afternoon even happened, like the sea did nothing at all.

Still Ward can't leave the beach, not yet. The other kids

have gone, last to leave of all of them, trying to get Ward to come on in with him, was Alex, come on, man, don't stay here now, come back with me . . . But Ward just needs to stay. The water continues to lie there, the colour slowly draining from the sand, the sea's silver surface, shadows forming as the sun holds its last colours in the sky . . .

His mother comes then.

'I heard,' she says. She walks up to Ward, where he's still sitting on the sand. 'What happened out there?' she says. 'I'm going in the car to be with him but . . .', and she's close enough now that Ward could touch her, 'I wanted to see you first.' Then she kneels down beside him, puts her arms around him.

Her bikini is still damp, like maybe she's been swimming, gone out on her own maybe, sometime this afternoon, somewhere long and far enough away that she knew nothing until now about what's been going on here . . . And how can that be? That all this time Ward's mother could be so far away? And yet, she has been, somewhere on her own and nowhere near this place, far enough that she never saw the wave, I think, or dreamed what the wave might do, and now is back here beside him.

'Come here . . .'

Her skin is warm, her stomach flat against her son's cheek as she holds him, and the damp fabric of her swimsuit against his skin as she cradles him in her arms and . . . I don't know. It's like . . . All of it . . . The morning, the noon. The girl. The gull's cry. And Alex, of course, Alex, and the party, and the wave come in . . . Like all of it . . . Is come back here in the body of the mother who holds her child in her arms. Like the sound of the sea Ward still carries in him, the memory of that great pulse, the boom, his father's gun and then pointed at his own head . . . Someone saying to him before: From now on you can always remember this: you saved your father's life. All of it, all of it . . . Come to rest here, in her . . . The letters in the sand.

When he's got the time, later, in his life, to think about all this stuff, it's how it might seem, that all of it is gathered up this moment, this moment now with Ward here with his mother and her murmuring 'Oh, oh, oh' to him as she strokes his hair. Saying 'My little boy', over and over, and needing to say it because it's not true, he's no longer that little boy, he'll never be that little boy again, but still she needs to say it, maybe, because it's her last chance. To hold him, comfort him, last chance. Taking her son's face in her hands as though to kiss him, to be close to him as she was close to him once when he was so small that his whole head could rest in the palm of her hand . . . Then she takes those hands away. She moves away, melts. The sun glints last, slips down. Dark comes.

*

Later, and the party is still going on. Like Ward thought would happen, Beth's parents not coming back so why stop a good thing. It broke up for a while there, with the accident, and who'd ever think Rob McFarlane would go down in the water, but an ambulance after all and someone said his leg was broken up down the length and that the cut he got off the side of the board's going to be with him forever.

'Really, you did a great thing, Ward,' says Richard, coming up to him now with a beer in his hand. 'If you hadn't seen your dad . . .'

'Yeah, just think . . .' Jeff whistles through his teeth. 'If you hadn't seen him . . .'

'What would have happened then.'

'What would have happened.'

'Yeah.'

Ward stands. They're all here. Same crowd, kind of drifted outside to the beach in front of Beth's place and someone has built a fire. The orange colours of it reach up like ribbons into the black sky. He shivers. Maybe it's the swim he took before, after his mother left him, and thinking now, at this moment, how it was to go back into the water. Maybe. Or just the fire here, all gold and red and yellow against the black. Who knows. Either way, the sea was as lovely as ever when he went back in, though she wanted to have him today, no doubt about it, then changed her mind and it was his dad instead and then she let him go . . .

He looks at his watch, past ten. His father will be sleeping now, with hospital gauze down the side of his face, his body, his leg in bits of bone but injected against the pain and there will be his mother sitting beside him on a little chair. And Ward did go swimming, all the way to the Eastern Bays and then back and the sun had gone down by then but to do it was like to clean himself. From his father's blood and vomit, kind of, and from his mother's hands . . . And the sea did clean him, would become an ocean for him that way, taking from him everything he needed to be taken. I think he knew that, Ward did, guessed it, before he went in, that the sea would let him begin again that way, be like a continent of land he could lose himself in but water, only water. In time he'd swum out to where the shelf drops, way out there, then he went on round past the point . . . Just swimming in the sea was all it was but the thing is, he never swims, not really, not without it having some reason to it, to check the current, take a board . . . But he has a feeling now all that's going to change. Standing here by this great fire, cold in his bones from the swim but warm . . . You can start with that. On this darkened beach, this evening when he came back here, arrived dripping out of the water and alone in the dark like on an unfamiliar shore . . .

And how he came in onto the beach then and gathered his shorts up off the cold sand, went home and there was no one there. How the house was dark. How Ward walked in, the front door open but the rooms dark and open to the evening and the table in the kitchen empty, and the chairs. He walked through all the rooms then, like taking possession is how it might have looked. He saw himself reflected in the long mirror that hung beside the fireplace in the sitting room and he looked like a man. Then he went through to the bathroom and started running the shower.

When he came out, steam around him like a covering . . . I can see, of course I can, how it was in him by then, the change, and it could only continue. He went through to the kitchen, naked, and stood dripping by the fridge while he looked inside. There was milk,

bread, half a roasted chicken his mother had left standing there, black chocolate, some kind of a pie. There
was melon, some cheese. Ward ate everything, standing
with the fridge door open and the light shining from it
the only light in the house. Like a man deprived of
food, standing naked and eating it all down. That kind
of a man. Naked and dripping and devouring everything he could see to eat in his mother's kitchen, in his
father's kitchen, in their house. He ate until he was full
and he drank a pint of milk, then he went through to
his room, dressed, and went out to rejoin the party he'd
left before.

That's exactly how it was. How he walked towards Beth's
house, the little road turning into grass under his feet,
heard the music, voices . . . Saw them all outside . . .

'Hey Wardy!'

'The man!'

And okay he might shiver a little but really, he's not
cold, he's been in the sea but he's come out of the sea
and is with the others now, entered into their circle of
the fire.

'Hey,' they said, and they were all talking to him,
about the afternoon, about his father.

'Hey.'

'Hey.'

He'd stood for a while with them, talking, and that

was fine and then he broke off, away from Richard, and that friend of his, Jeff, the girls from before, and that was fine too, picking up a beer from the pile and going back onto the grass and up onto Beth's porch and Alex was there.

'You.'

Just Alex, no one else.

'I saw the whole thing,' he says, he shakes his head. 'You're a piece of work, you know?'

Ward smiles a little.

'My dad's binoculars. We all came out. It was later, I mean . . .'

'I don't know what the time was,' Ward says.

'When you left, but Richard came out, saw the wave. Man, that's what we were looking at when we saw you guys . . . And you . . .' He shakes his head again. 'You were awesome out there.'

'It was my dad who was first,' Ward says. 'I only followed –'

'C'mon.' Alex looks at him, that little kind of Alex look. No sunglasses now. No bits of water flicking at him. Just looking, right into Ward's eyes and holding his eyes in his eyes. 'I know what I saw,' he says then. 'What we all saw.'

'Well . . .' Ward turns away, but Alex won't let him, he takes his arm.

'Seriously,' he says. He holds his arm.

'Oh yeah, seriously . . .'

'No,' Alex says. 'I mean it.' He holds Ward's arm tighter, tighter, and with his other hand grabs Ward's other arm, so he's holding him and looking at him . . . And for a second there's this moment, as they both look at each other, like they're a reflection of each other, these two, like that moment before when they were together on the beach . . . And then Jenny comes up, puts her arm around Alex's waist and he turns. 'Hey!' he says to her, and he lets go of Ward then, puts his arm around her waist and they both go off together.

Ward sits awhile. The voices are all still there out in the summer night, and somewhere his parents are, miles away, together in the hospital room, like they've always been together, always will be . . . And Ward's here and there are all kinds of feelings and thoughts, who knows . . . But the air is sweet, in this place they all love, with grass and clean sand and the salt, the clean wind that comes in to take all the feelings away.

'Guys! Take it –'

'Eas-eee.'

So he hears the voices, where they'll always be, out there, but Ward has the sense of the weight of his body on the soft wood of Beth's parents' porch where he sits, the springy summer grass dry under his feet and sand

and this world, it's true, is beautiful to be alive in, to be clean in. It's beautiful here.

There's a movement, softness beside him and a girl's voice.

'Hi Ward.'

Alison steps out of the dark.

'I wanted to find you here,' she says. 'I wanted to see you again.' She smiles, puts out her hand.

'Me too,' Ward says. He puts out his hand to take hers and she sits down next to him, side by side, their bodies nearly touching. They don't look at each other, only out at all that's before them and, you know, there's nothing to say, nothing Ward feels he has to say, just the sound of the sea, out there somewhere in the dark, and then Alison turns her face towards him.

'Hello,' she says to him, so quiet it's a whisper, and Ward turns to her, her face like a moon on the sea's dark surface.

'Hello,' he says.

Late afternoon

For the sea, for now, the time is done. She pulls back, she can rest, slip back to the place where she came from, and the boys, all the boys . . .

Let them go.

There's the sound of the sea, the waters folding away, the tide gone . . . Into distance, light, to where the sun is now but disappearing slowly from our sight . . .

You know that feeling. Like standing alone someplace, trees around you maybe and their shade to cover, and your friends, the kids you know seem far away . . . That's how the sea seems, I think, when you look at her this time of day. Like she's there but apart too, pulled back into her own private place, and where she comes from, where she goes . . .

137

Like a story, when the story's done . . .

You sense her more than see her.

Slipping back into past time, and only some pieces come forward to remember, to start over, the next story, and the next . . .
   That's what the sea's like, the sea says,
   Like this story . . .

But the writing's fading already as the sun melts down into water, like words written on the sand and already a wave comes in to take them, smoothes the letters away. Even the name Ward wrote before, C–a–r–o . . . his mother, the sea has come to claim those letters too, the last of her gone into water now.

She said goodbye to her son and went to be with her husband, sit by his hospital bed.
   'What went on out there this afternoon?' she'll say, and he'll do something, maybe make a motion with his hand like, How crazy was I? And then whisper later, 'I don't know what I've been doing . . .' while with her fingers his wife presses tears away from his eyes.

That's one ending, another already written. Either way . . .

Just writing on the sand.

It is, it all is, and yet it also . . . Is it all. The story of a boy, of his day here, his friends . . . There's a father, his wife . . . And the sea . . . More than anything else, the sea . . .

And I won't ever change, says that story, as she slips back into the deep.

Tomorrow, with the first frail light of dawn she'll come back again, come creeping gently in upon the sand, but in the meantime there's a fire to burn on the beach and the boy who's not a boy may shiver but he's not cold or afraid or alone even in all this emptiness around him, this place in the world with its sweet curve of coastline, faded grasses . . .

That's the feeling.
We're left with here.
The story here. But listen . . .

Shhh . . .

No more words now, only

Shhh . . .

The sound of the sea in the distance, in the coming night.

Shhh, as she falls away.

Shhh.

Shhh.

Shhh.